Praise for *Summer Girls*

"*Summer Girls* is a powerful, haunting, moving book — equal parts poetry and thriller. If Alissa Nutting, Mary Gaitskill, and Emma Cline frankensteined a baby, it might feel something like this. You will not come away unscathed."

—Richard Thomas, Bram Stoker, Shirley Jackson, and Thriller Award finalist

"Fans of true crime will love *Summer Girls*. Reading it feels like studying an old Poloroid photo for too long, its faded colors and scratches revealing the flaws of nostalgia. Trent's introspective prose will gut you in a way no other beach read can."

—Rebecca Jones-Howe, author of *Ending In Ashes* and *Vile Men*

"*Summer Girls* is one of those novels I'm always searching for: unsettling, psychologically revelatory, and as smart as it is suspenseful, both a coming-of-age novel and a dark mystery that builds toward an explosive climax. I won't soon forget these sisters, their stumbling progress toward adulthood, or the sinister but magnetic characters who shape their fates."

—Holly Goddard Jones, author of *The Next Time You See Me* and *Antipodes: Stories*

Summer Girls

Letitia Trent

Haunted Doll
House

BINGHAMTON, NY

Copyright © 2024 by Letitia Trent
All rights reserved

Cover art and author photograph by Letita Trent
Images appear by kind permission

Published by Haunted Doll House, an imprint of Agape Editions
Editor: Fox Henry Frazier
Design: Sarah Reck

Library of Congress
Cataloguing-in-Publication Data

Summer Girls // Letitia Trent

Library of Congress Control Number 2024941307

Trent, Letitia
ISBN 978-1-7364655-7-8

9 8 7 6 5 4 3 2 1
FIRST EDITION

Content Warning

This book contains depictions of mutually inebriated sexual activity between teenagers, death due to cancer, alcoholism, absentee parents, grooming, statutory rape, abduction, coercive control, attempted murder, suicide, verbal and psychological abuse, gaslighting, cults, cult behavior, brainwashing, physical/sexual abuse, and references to murder. It may contain other potentially triggering topics or subject matter not listed here. Please prioritize your own well-being when choosing to interact with any potentially triggering topics.

For my sister. We got out.

I

January, 2017

I knew somebody was coming long before I could see them.

We live so far out that I can hear a car turning down our gravel drive from the main road, there's no ambient noise but the wind and the birds to muffle the sound. When any vehicle approaches, our dog Watson takes notice, barking with his head between the curtains until I come to him and soothe him, let him know there's no real danger, it's just the mail or the closest neighbor coming to ask if I want to buy a rick of firewood. In the winter, it's even worse — the ice crackling all around us after a storm, exploding from branches in sub-zero temperatures, trees breaking from the weight of ice and frozen snow. The bursts of noise set Watson on edge, making him bounce around the room, barking to be let out to protect us from the danger, whatever the danger might be.

When the vehicle became visible through the bare birches, I saw a black, featureless SUV, like something an FBI agent from a movie might drive.

I didn't imagine I'd done anything wrong — I'd spent the

last six months almost entirely in the house, breastfeeding and rewatching old television shows and reading books I hadn't touched since college. My mind went instead to Mariah.

They're here to tell me she's dead, I thought, and then tried to banish the thought. I hadn't heard from her in months, but that didn't mean she was dead. She'd been absent for over a year in the past, and I'd never had that thought before. I attributed my new awareness of everyone's mortality to the baby. I could barely imagine my husband driving down the mountain to town without seeing him fly off the road, shredding the flimsy guardrails that stood between him and the pine forest valley below. Every time we ventured from the house, I could imagine myself on a future episode of *I Survived*, detailing how I'd lost everyone I loved in some freak disaster and was the only one left standing, almost as a kind of punishment.

This time, Watson began to howl as he had when a black bear had waddled up to our yard from the forest, trying in vain to open our chained trash cans. I picked the baby up from her nest of blankets and toys on the floor. She'd started crying, too, only increasing Watson's fear. I hushed her and the dog, who I held by the collar and dragged to the nearest bathroom. He wasn't a friendly dog, and I liked that about him, but I didn't need him assaulting people emerging from black, unmarked cars, probably with concealed weapons somewhere in their boxy jackets.

"Shhhh, Faun," I cooed into the baby's ear. She cooed back and reached up to touch my face. My husband Colin was at work. I glanced at my phone on the kitchen counter and considered texting him a quick message, but I didn't. Sometimes, there's a part of me that wants to keep the most important things private from him, from everyone. Besides, if it was about Mariah, I wanted to handle it myself. I could keep my composure on my own. Colin standing there, asking me how I *feel* about everything, would only make it harder.

I opened the front door.

"Mrs. Clarke?" A man in an unadorned black suit asked. He held out a badge, which I did not read, only registered as authority.

My heart beat faster. "Yes."

"My name is Agent Wheeler, and this is Agent Collier." He pointed to the woman next to him, her badge also out. In her photo, her hair was shorter and her lipstick redder, but she was still the same polished, almost gleaming woman. He looked exactly like his photo, down to the precise part in his hair and the smooth face, as though he'd just shaved with a straight razor before he arrived at my door.

"We're here to ask you some questions about your sister, Mariah Price."

"What's happened to her?" I asked. "Is she okay?"

Both detectives looked at me blankly.

"That's what we're here to find out," The other detective said. "We can't seem to locate her and would like to ask her some questions. We thought maybe you could help."

How I would have loved to help Mariah, but it had been years since she'd let me do anything but watch from a distance as she rushed into darkness, getting farther and farther away from me.

May, 1999

I got the idea of Mariah and I spending the summer with Aunt Bobbie right after my high school graduation.

We'd pulled ourselves together for the event, us Price girls. When the principal called my name, *Chelsea Price*, I walked up to the podium unsteadily in my mother's heels (a size too big and slipping from my feet with each step), my cheap, flowered dress beneath the polyester robe swishing against my naked legs. I waved to my mother and Bobbie and they waved back, both dressed in their best, holding hands.

Mom and Bobbie did not always get along. Sometimes Mom would call her a bitch when she was irritated with something accurate Bobbie'd said about how much she had been drinking, for example, but they loved each other. Mom had even gone up to stay with Bobbie for several weeks after her longtime girlfriend, Cassandra, had died of lymphoma. That was two years ago, and Bobbie still lived alone in the enormous farmhouse that she and my mom had grown up in, just three miles from the Atlantic. In the two years since Cassandra's death, both women had changed.

By the time I was a senior in high school, Mom was mostly

out of good days. She spent the majority of the time in her room, coming down for soda refills and the occasional food or to do a grocery and liquor run. She barely ate meals and instead brought boxes of crackers and cases of generic cola up to her room and would live off of them for weeks. She was bony, but without muscle, her skin sallow and sagging. Bobbie had encouraged her to seek treatment for her drinking, but she'd refused. How could anyone treat my mother when she insisted so loudly and with such certainty that absolutely nothing was wrong but the whole fucking world being against her?

I stopped knowing how to talk to my mother that year. And then, we both stopped trying, moving warily around each other, though some nights when I didn't see her emerge from her room for several hours, I'd go up and make sure she hadn't drowned herself in the bathtub or choked on her own vomit. When I'd duck my head in, her room smelled stale and salty, but not yet rotten, though I knew that was coming soon. She was now officially a hoarder, her room crowded with vodka bottles and magazines in stacks and mountains of laundry. Some disaster was coming, and I didn't plan to be around when it happened.

But on that day, my graduation, everyone was together and Mom was sober, at least for a while. Back at the house, where Mom struggled with her shaky hands to get the plastic film off a tray of limp, bargain vegetables with a tub of lumpy ranch dressing in the middle, we all gathered in the low-lit living room. I hoped that the house didn't look too bad, didn't smell too strange, that Bobbie couldn't tell how bad things had gotten. As Bobbie settled in on the couch that we'd covered with an old quilt, hiding cigarette burns and food stains, I watched Mariah flitting around the room, talking excitedly to them. Mom's hands trembled as she tried to pour ranch dressing onto her plate and nod at Mariah at the same time, a task that took far more concentration than it should have. I watched Bobbie listen, but even as she did, I saw her surveying the room, noticing the dark corners full of piled magazines, the smell of trash bags in the dark corner of the kitchen wafting into the living room area.

When Mom and Mariah were seated in the living room, Bobbie gestured to me and said aloud, "Let's get some drinks for everyone." Mom looked up, and almost opened her mouth.

"Soda all around," Bobbie said, not giving Mom the chance to ask for something we'd all regret giving her. "We'll get it. Chelsea can show me the way." I could tell Mom wanted to stop us, but she couldn't figure out how to say it on the spot.

In the kitchen, I looked around fruitlessly for clean cups in the empty cupboards. I attempted to tackle the dishes overflowing in the sink, but Bobbie tapped me on the shoulder as I was trying to find the sink plug underneath a pot blackened with burnt eggs, and pulled me even deeper into the kitchen, toward the backdoor that led out to our deck crowded with bags full of cans and garbage.

"Tell me the truth," she said, "is your mom okay?"

I shook my head. "It's bad lately. As soon as you leave, she's gonna start drinking and won't stop till she passes out."

"How often is she like this?"

I shrugged, frustrated with the question, which implied maybe there was ever a respite. "All the time. Every night. For years now. You just never asked."

Bobbie didn't stop to feel offended or protest or call me out on my hasty words. In truth, she had asked, for years, until my mother had told her to stop butting into her business, so she had stopped, and then Cassandra had died.

She nodded. "You're right," she said. "I've been off in my own world for too long. You both need to come and stay with me this summer. Let's go out there and you bring it up. I'll support it, I'll say what I need to say to get your mom to agree. You both need some space, and maybe in that space, we can get her some help."

Her words were a relief. I felt as though she'd cut a heavy backpack from my shoulders. I had been worried about the summer, all that empty expanse of time, the heat of our house becoming suffocating when the window air conditioners stopped working, and Mom even less interested in the outside world than she'd been the year before.

We found a stockpile of red plastic cups in a tall cupboard, washed out the webbing and dead spiders, and filled each cup with soda and ice. As we passed out the drinks, I proposed a summer stay at Bobbie's house by the ocean.

"I figure I'll be away to college soon, so I might not have a chance to just spend a summer with my sister again," I said, handing Mariah her drink.

Mom hesitated at first, saying she couldn't take up Bobbie's time like that, she couldn't let us run wild and make Bobbie responsible.

"You remember how we used to be, Bobbie? How that

town was the perfect combination of boring and too damn much?"

Bobbie laughed. "These two aren't like us. They have better sense already."

Mom looked at me, then Mariah, and then nodded. "They do, don't they? Good girls already. Look at this one, graduated magna cum laude."

I shrugged. "It was summa." I didn't care much about my grades, but it bothered me to be singled out at all if it wasn't in first place.

"Still," she said, "I'm proud of you both." She gestured to Mariah, who came to her and fell into her hug. A rare thing anymore. I could scarcely believe the woman I was seeing that night, nearly lucid, nearly the woman she'd been years ago, when she had still been a functioning alcoholic. But it was getting late, and I didn't imagine she had much sober self left in her.

"So, do you think we could go, mom? I'd watch Mariah —"

Bobbie interrupted me. "Not your job, kid. I'll watch you both. It's no trouble. It gets lonely in that big house all by myself."

Everyone went silent at that. Bobbie had played her trump card. Mom agreed, and once Bobbie left, she gave us both a hard, lingering hug and went up to her room, where I found her when I came in just an hour later to check and make sure she was breathing, sound asleep, an empty bottle in her bed, the television whispering.

Despite my intention to stop, in the early days of that last summer at Aunt Bobbie's, I woke early to check on her, too. Those mornings I would make my way slowly up the wooden steps, the whole house echoing with the creaks and pops of the old wood. It was a classic New England farmhouse, sturdy and unadorned, the beams exposed, the floors and baseboards having long lost their original varnish. A slammed door would echo through the house like a gunshot, and you couldn't help but know that somebody was coming, the floor made such a racket. I'd tiptoe, hoping she couldn't hear me, and stand outside her room listening to see if she was snoring or stirring. If she wasn't, I'd open the door to make sure she was only asleep, watching her sheets for the subtle rising and falling, her face for some flutter of eyelid.

As soon as we'd arrived in June, I felt *something* was going to happen that summer. The form of something wasn't clear to me, but the world felt unstable the year I turned eighteen and never quite righted itself. For one thing, Bobbie was foggy and unfocused, not her usual sharp self, and I worried that she might be drifting away from us. Not the way Mom was, through an aggressive attempt at destroying herself, but by willing herself away from engagement with the world, more and more, until I thought maybe one morning I'd find an empty bed.

When Mom dropped us off, her hands shaking so fiercely from the morning she'd taken off of drinking that I worried she'd run us off the road, I noticed for the first time how Bobbie's house stood back from the street, protected in a little pocket of trees (hers was the last house on the street, abutting a park). We were close enough to smell the sea, to taste it on our lips and bare arms by the end of a long day of being outside, but far enough away to be tucked into a leafy forest.

"You girls know I love you, right?" Mom said, the question too insistent, her shaky hands clawing for my shoulder to pull me close for a kiss that smelled like mouthwash and some sharp, unconcealable rot. We told her we did and eagerly dragged our wheel-less suitcases away from the car. I was worried she'd give in and drink before the half-hour drive back home was over but also worried that if she didn't give in, she'd have a seizure and fly off the highway. I tried to remember I only had to be here, that this was about me and Mariah surviving, about mom getting herself together. I walked across the lush, springy grass, one foot after the other. I had to let go of worrying about her dying. I could do nothing about it, and worrying only made me miserable.

So in that first week, I borrowed Bobbie's bike and went daily into town, applying in person to every restaurant and shop and convenience store position I could find, calling random numbers posted on electrical poles and tacked to the corkboard outside the coffeeshop. I was relieved to quickly land a job as a hostess at a semi-fancy seafood restaurant right on the water, held up on steady beams so the expansive porch extended out over the rocky shore. I must have made a good impression, because the manager asked me to come in the next day and shadow the current hostess, who was pregnant and preparing to ship off back to whatever small, landlocked town she'd come from before she'd tried to make it out here, only to get impregnated by a visiting musician in a Bruce Springsteen tribute band.

"He didn't even sing, he just played the bass," the manager whispered while we watched her struggle to maneuver her stomach around closely packed tables.

"People think because it's a vacation town that they'll always feel like they're on vacation if they live here," she shook her head just thinking about this folly. "What living here does is suck all the vacation out of you." I watched the pregnant hostess press against the small of her back as she listened to a couple complain about the wait time and felt a momentary doubt: maybe I would end up being the same old person in this new place, only saddled with a pregnancy or a bad relationship or debt or whatever else a person could accumulate while trying to get away from where they came from. That thought quickly evaporated, though. I was not then capable of seeing myself as the same kind of person as this greasy, exhausted woman with unidentifiable food stains on her shirtfront.

After the interview, I stepped out onto the enormous deck that extended over the water and watched the cold sea lap. This place was beautiful, in a spare way, with all the rocky, treeless shorelines and the ocean, that big body of changeability, lining the horizon, but it wasn't an easy place — Bobbie often complained of the repairs she had to make after a nor'easter blew down her sheds or the shingles from the roof. The unpredictability appealed to me. Some mornings you'd wake up and throw on a skirt over a bathing suit because it was so hot and end up wearing a sweater and thick, woolen socks by bedtime. I liked the smell of fish that permeated the air and I liked the idea of folding myself into this historic old building, a place where all the linen-clad summer people murmured into their clams and lobster over candles as they hung in safety above the brutal shore.

The job itself seemed easy. All I had to do was make people

feel special and noticed and make myself disappear into the room when my work was over — I couldn't mess up if I remembered that my sole purpose was to make them feel as though I cared, but not too much. After my first night of shadowing, the manager said I was a natural.

"You might end up with my job someday," she told me, tapping her nametag, where it said *Shelly*, and *Manager* below it. She told me that she had started on as a hostess years ago and had worked her way up to management. "Twenty years I had jobs like yours, and I was damned good at them, until the day they replaced me with a younger girl. Then, I knew I had to get myself into the back room, where nobody cared if my hair got gray or my ass got wide."

The look I gave her must have translated as fear, because she reached out to touch my shoulder, reassuringly.

"Oh, but honey, you have a lot of years left in this uniform, if that's where you want to be."

I wasn't worried about getting too old to be a hostess. I was worried about getting stuck in this vacation town for so long that I might never leave. As much as I liked visiting Bobbie and wanted to get away from home, it wasn't far enough away from where I'd come from to truly feel free. I was close enough to consider making my way back home if I failed. Eventually, I'd have to get myself so far from home that failure wasn't possible anymore.

I arrived at Bobbie's that night to find Mariah waiting for

me in the living room, vibrating with excitement. Mariah at fifteen was such a strange, kind kid. Everybody said so: her report cards in elementary school had always said *conscientious, a good classroom helper* but also *daydreamy, distractible, has a difficult time connecting with her peers*. The last three years she'd let her blonde hair grow long from the previous rough bowl cut I'd given her, so long it touched her elbows, so long it ratted up into an impossible tangle when she didn't carefully brush it each morning and evening. She was wearing a nightgown dotted with violets and her feet were bare. Her fingernails were dirty but painted a bright, cheap pink that seemed innocent on her, trashy and ridiculous on me when I tried the same hue for my first day of work.

We hugged as soon as I walked through the door, delighted by each other's presence, even at fifteen and eighteen years old, which people have since told me is not the usual way teenage sisters feel about each other.

"I got a job!"

She clapped, and then blurted out "I got one, too! I talked to the neighbors, the new ones with kids. They were all out in the yard playing and I just went over to introduce myself. They told me they're here because they both got grants for making art, they plan to be here for a year at least."

"Art," I repeated. "Like, they have a job making art?"

She shrugged. "They teach art at some college and are artists, too. They're going to let me have meals over there and I'll take care of the kids while they work. They'll pay me extra to watch the kids if they ever want to go out on dates on weekends."

The neighbors had moved in not long after we'd arrived.

We'd watched the bustle from Bobbie's living room windows as movers carried boxes into the two-story cape cod house next door, which had stood empty for years, Bobbie told us. *Probably the heating costs*, she'd said, *all those windows.* The saltbox roof and enormous chimney of gaudy red brick made it impractical as well as inconspicuous, according to Bobbie, who had a very New England horror of houses that seemed to be showing off. I liked it, though.

"It makes me think of a cottage in the woods in a movie or something," Mariah had said. "It looks kinda like it's all put together with different parts that don't fit."

I agreed. It did look like something out of a story.

Out of the moving truck had emerged threadbare furniture and box after battered box. And then, from a car, came three children, all under the age of twelve, and two adults. The woman wore a yellow maxi dress, ungathered at the waist, the hem dragging the ground. My first thought when I saw her was that she looked like a bright ghost against that dark green yard.

The father had long, black hair that he'd tied back in a low ponytail. The more I watched them, the more it became clear the adults were older than they first looked, in their early forties at least, But they *felt* young.

I told Mariah about my job at the restaurant. "I'm gonna be the hostess."

"Sounds perfect," she said. I showed her my polyester slacks and button-up shirt with a yellowing collar and threadbare cuffs.

"I think this outfit comes from 1975," I said, sliding my fingers along the thick, slippery fabric of the slacks. My fingertips came away slightly greasy, smelling faintly of plastic.

"Put it on!" Mariah insisted, so I did, walking across the wooden floors carefully to avoid waking Bobbie up, pretending to be on a catwalk. The pants fit tight around my stomach, creating a bulge, and the blouse gapped at the breast, revealing the sad little bow at the center of my bra, but still, I felt adult, professional. Mariah clapped for me as I turned on my sock feet, spinning.

We celebrated our jobs by drinking a bottle of champagne that Mariah had found in the back of Bobbie's liquor cabinet, a bottle so dusty we both figured she'd never know we'd taken it.

"I hate stealing from her," Mariah said, "but I don't think she was the one who drank, so she'll never miss it." It certainly seemed as though most of the cabinet had been untouched in the two years since Cassandra had died.

Mariah and I had been stealing liquor for years. Mom had so much hidden around the house that she never missed it, and we didn't feel bad drinking her alcohol. More for us meant less for her, which was the only way we could slow her down. Usually, if she ran completely out of booze, she'd just fall asleep, so we figured the more we drank, the more she'd sleep, the more likely it would be that she'd wake up clear and well instead of foggy and sick.

As we drank the lukewarm sparkling wine, Mariah told me about the family next door, consisting of Willow and Stefan, the parents, and the children, River, Sage, and Persephone. Willow and Stefan were both artists on leave from university jobs, hoping to work on their projects in the peace of a small town. Stefan had gotten some grant that allowed them to rent the house and stay home all summer and the following fall and winter, until they had to return to their university jobs.

"He got some genius grant," Mariah said. "I can tell he was kind of embarrassed to say it, but Willow told me what it was. She's really proud of him. They seem so happy with each other, and still in love." Mariah paused to drink warm champagne straight from the bottle.

I felt like a slacker compared to Mariah, who had not only gotten a job but also spent time getting to know new people. She already seemed different, more mature.

This is good, I told myself. This is exactly what this summer is supposed to be about, becoming more adult, more independent. She would need to be independent once she got home and started her sophomore year without me, if Mom continued to decline, as I imagined she would. She'd have to learn how to take care of herself until I could make enough money to have her come live with me. When I thought about college, I didn't imagine living in a dorm room or going to a keg party or joining a sorority, I imagined juggling a job and school for the purpose of getting an even better job, and, as quickly as possible, having Mariah come live with me.

"What's being a hostess like?" Mariah asked, passing me the bottle.

"I bring people to their tables. I don't have to remember orders or try to balance plates. I just have to look neat and be friendly and keep track of who goes where. Seems like a pretty good gig to me."

"Any cool people there?"

I shrugged. I had scoped out the other employees for a new Jason, the guy from my high school that I had been seeing casually senior year. I wanted somebody cute but temporary, hopefully less interested in poisonous snakes and switchblades than the old Jason had been. The day I'd told him I was leaving, he was close to tears, though he tried to hide it.

"Sucks that you're leaving, man." He'd said, ducking his head and running his hands through his hair, a gesture I'd come to know from moments he had to admit he didn't have enough money for weed and needed to borrow some. "I guess this was just a temporary thing?"

I'd been shocked by the question. I had thought that was clear from the beginning. I had never attempted to take him seriously.

"Uh, yeah," I answered. "I was always going to college. I'm not staying here."

"You think I am?" He'd asked, hurt by the implication.

"I mean, yeah. I thought you were keeping your job over at the grocery store?" He was a stocker now, but had just been promoted to the meat department, where he'd learn how to use the grinder, slice ham, and otherwise shape meat into the bloodless, cling-wrapped lumps.

"It's not forever," he said, ducking his head again, his mood turning from chagrined to angry.

"You love it there," I pointed out, trying to touch his shoulder, wanting to be more soft with him. His reaction was such a shock that I hadn't prepared myself to speak more gently or consider potential hurt feelings.

He shrugged away my touch. "Fuck you," was all he could manage before walking away.

I felt guilty for misleading him without realizing it and tried to arrange a going away dinner for us, but he stood me up, which I admit I deserved. I hadn't meant to treat him carelessly, I had just never considered the idea that I could mean anything to him or anyone else. I wasn't even a whole person yet. I assumed everyone else saw me through the same lens of inadequacy.

The only guy at the restaurant who'd looked promising was Jackson, the dishwasher who also took out the trash at the end of the day. I met him out by the dumpsters, where the smokers gathered. It was my usual way of making friends. I only smoked at work — I didn't really like smoking itself, but I liked smokers. They had a hint of desperation that I appreciated, and they had a reason to be gathered together, which helped with small talk. So I started to smoke, casually, usually inhaling nothing. But at this restaurant, he was the only other smoker out there, which surprised me: you could usually count on the poor people doing the shittiest work to keep up the fine tradition of smoking behind restaurants.

Jackson's hair was curly with sweat and humidity, his white t-shirt stained with sweat, but I liked the smell of him, tobacco and salt and traces of deodorant. I told him some of the story, about staying with my aunt Bobbie and graduating from high school and turning eighteen just a few weeks before, but I didn't mention my mom. In what I left out, I might have made it seem like we were from this town and not natives of a town a half hour inland, known for its empty factories and skyrocketing crime rate. I didn't feel bad misleading Jackson. He was just practice. I wouldn't endear myself to him more than I had to, I'd be just enough to interest him but never give him enough to create more complicated feelings. I imagined there was a recipe to this, and if I could just make it out, I could pluck whatever I needed from experience and leave nobody hurt.

Mariah and I drank the entire bottle and wanted more. She was giddy, talking breathlessly about the family next door and the art in their house.

"Willow makes these wild things out of fabric, like dolls with missing faces or extra arms. They're really cool and scary," Mariah said, pouring me a glass of some green liquid from a bottle missing its label.

"This might kill us," I said, but took a swig anyway. It tasted like Nyquil and burned my tongue.

"Jesus. What even is this?"

Mariah shrugged and grabbed the bottle, taking a drink without hesitation. Her eyes widened and she immediately spit it back into the bottle, sputtering.

"Yikes. You're not wrong."

I took the bottle to the kitchen and buried it deep in the trash. I grabbed another, more promising bottle from the back of the cabinet, something supposedly tasting of oranges and amaretto and handed it to Mariah, who was dabbing globs of green liquid from her nightgown.

"I hope I get to meet them sometime," I said, gesturing toward the window, where the neighbor's house still burned bright in almost every window.

Mariah dropped her attempts to clean up. "Oh, I forgot to say, they've invited us over for dinner on Sunday! You don't work then, right?"

I shook my head. "What do you think I should wear?"

I had nothing but work clothes and t-shirts and jeans and threadbare tank tops and shorts.

"One of my dresses," Mariah said. "you'll look positively *otherworldly*."

"I don't think I could ever be otherworldly. That's you."

Mariah laughed. As a kid, she'd been obsessed with fairies. She'd been Tinkerbell for three consecutive Halloweens ages six through nine. Later, she loved stories about mermaids, about creatures that weren't quite human, that got to come into the world in human form and then retreat back when somebody stumbled on their secret or broke their trust. We would watch *The Little Mermaid* and she would make us stop just before Ariel traded her voice for her legs. She liked Ariel under the sea and longing for a prince better than Ariel with her prince, getting married and becoming some regular woman married to a regular man.

We drank together until the amaretto and orange drink (sickly sweet, but somehow comforting, like the liquid version of something you'd find in a grandma's candy bowl) was gone and then stumbled upstairs and fell into an immediate and heavy sleep.

June, 1999

I stood next to Mariah in their doorway and couldn't help but feel like I was already a disappointment. I was wearing Mariah's gauziest, prettiest, itchiest dress and regretted not noticing how sheer it was until I stood in the light of their doorstep and looked down to see my legs, shadowy beneath the white fabric. The dress wasn't my style at all and I didn't know how to move in it. I was cold, and rashes of goosebumps traveled up and down my arms and legs. I held a bottle of Bobbie's wine, this time wine we'd asked for, to bring to dinner.

"Should teenagers bring wine to dinner?" Bobbie had asked when we requested it.

"It's a gift for them, Bobbie," Mariah had said, rolling her eyes, but with a gentle mockery, and Bobbie had shrugged and nodded, instructing us to pick a white.

"You're invited, too," Mariah said, though I could tell she hoped Bobbie would say no. As much as we loved her, we knew we couldn't exactly be ourselves with her there.

She waved her hand at us, dismissing the idea. Bobbie wasn't a big socializer. She liked her house and her family and not much else. She'd worked for years in accounting, a solitary job that had atrophied her social skills, at least according to Cassandra, who had lovingly teased her about her hermity ways for years.

"You look amazing," Mariah assured me. She'd given me one long braid down the left side of my head, framing my face, but the rest of my hair hung loose like hers. We'd used a red lipstick we found in the shared upstairs bathroom to stain our cheeks and lips, which emphasized the natural flush I already had at the thought of meeting these glamorous people. I worried that I looked like I had a fever.

That night, the air was cool and carried the salty residue of the sea, touching everything with salt and a buzzy, electric feeling of movement.

Stefan opened the door to greet us. He wore a linen shirt, sky blue, opened down the front, exposing his chest. He had an alarming nest of curly, black hair. I was taken aback at how much of him I was seeing. I didn't know any men who revealed their chests, or their smiles, that casually. I stepped back and Mariah stepped forward, taking the bottle from my hand.

"We brought this," Mariah said, holding it out to him.

"Wonderful!" He shouted. He held out his hand and grabbed mine, pulling me up the steps behind Mariah and through the door. His touch was firm. I hadn't often been touched, not by a man, definitely not by an adult man. Jason had always touched me tentatively. Perhaps he could feel me withdrawing from him even as I allowed him to pull me close. If Stefan felt any hesitation from me, he didn't show it or even seem to register it.

The house had a mudroom, where galoshes were piled

up and coats hung on hooks. Mariah led the way as he whisked us through the dim entryway to the light of the living room. It smelled alive in there, like rain and dogs and cooking, and soon enough, the dogs introduced themselves, bounding in from a darkened hallway where one of the children had released them, barking at us until Stefan calmed them with a word and touch to their heads. He released my hand and I rubbed the place where I'd felt the pressure.

"Your sister is a blessing to us," he told me over the whining of the dogs. "The children already love her. We already love her. What's your name again?"

"Chelsea," I said. I looked for Mariah, but she'd slipped away from me, gone to the kitchen to help Willow with the cooking.

"Come on out and meet Chelsea!" Stefan called into the kitchen, and a woman came out, dressed in red, her hair loose around her shoulders. She brought a smell of oranges: it surrounded me when she hugged me tight, which, to my surprise, almost made me cry, that strong, motherly hug that I hadn't felt in a very long time. I didn't like how much I was feeling already during what was supposed to be a simple dinner.

"These girls are both like nymphs," she said, turning to Stefan. "Can't you see them, crawling from the heart of an enormous tree?"

Stefan regarded me critically, as though determining the truth of this statement.

"This one came out of the forest," he said. "The other one crawled from the water."

"You're right," Willow said. She turned, all of her warmth trained on me. "This one has her feet buried in the ground. You must let me paint you in a scene," she said. "I have a commission for the cover of this fantasy book, not the kind of thing I usually do but the author is a genius, she's taken the genre to new places. It's got nymphs in it. I figured I'd put one on the front. Will you be my nymph?"

She reached out to me, brushing her fingers across my cheeks as she tucked my hair behind my ears, and didn't wait for me to answer.

"I like your haircolor. Is it blonde or brown? A little red in the light and dull in the dark. Wavy but not curly. It's an in-between thing, red and brown and blonde all at once, liminal just like you."

She was talking to herself now, planning the painting, seeing me as a collection of colors and shapes and meanings.

"It would be cool to be painted," I lied, squirming away from her hands. "But I have a job that keeps me out pretty late…" The idea of being a painting on the cover of a book made me feel both very special and very embarrassed. At the time, embarrassment always won.

She waved her hand at me, dismissing my concerns.

"We don't keep regular hours over here anyway," she said. "We can make it work."

The children came out and saved me from talking about it more or embarrassing myself further. River was the oldest, skinny with blonde hair brushing his shoulders. He held out a book, an out-of-date encyclopedia.

"Look what I made," he said, and opened up the book to show his mother how he'd blacked out words, cut the pages, and remade them into poems and collages.

"It's beautiful," she said.

He nodded and turned to a page halfway through the book. "This chapter is just words that start with the letter M."

She looked at me, shaking her head. "We got him the O.U.L.I.P.O manifesto for Christmas last year and he can't stop making constraint-based poems."

I had no idea what she was talking about, but I nodded.

Sage was the middle one, around eight. He was big-eyed and shy and hung behind the other two. The youngest, Persephone, was four. She asked me my name and tugged at my dress.

"Chelsea," I told her.

"Will you visit like Mariah does? Mariah plays dolls with me."

"I will sometime," I told her. "I'd love to play dolls."

She nodded. "My dolls are artists, like Mom."

"That makes sense."

I tried to imagine what it would have been like to grow up in this family, one where the dolls could be artists and the books were so plentiful that you could tear them apart, as though your own words could be as important as the words in books, and nobody would get mad about it. I couldn't tell if Stefan and Willow just had a lot of money or if they simply didn't care about things the way regular people did.

We all made our way to the kitchen, dogs and kids and

adults, and sat down to a spaghetti dinner, served on mismatched plates with forks and spoons and knives of all different sizes. Willow brought out two loaves of bread, freshly baked, and pulled them apart with her hands, giving us each enormous hunks. Bowls of olive oil, peppered and salted, were placed between every two dishes. I was supposed to share it with River, who dug into his bread and spaghetti immediately. I felt uncomfortable with this, sitting around a table with people I didn't know, eating with them, sharing a bowl. I was used to eating alone in my room, usually in front of the television, or in the kitchen by myself, Mom upstairs watching muted crime shows with the closed captioning on because she had a migraine and any amount of noise would set her howling. This dinner table was loud and messy and together, like something from a movie. Persephone fed a dog under the table. Every time River took a hunk of bread from our shared loaf, I did as well, taking it as a cue that I was allowed to eat, too.

Mariah sat across from me, next to Willow. She was animated, her cheeks red. I saw she'd gotten a glass of wine — I wondered if Willow had noticed. Stefan, who was seated on the other side of me, noticed my glance.

"Mariah," I said, leaning toward her, trying to keep my voice down, "I don't think Bobbie would want us drinking."

"I just had a few sips," she said.

Stefan watched our exchange. "I'm sorry," he said, "I didn't even notice she'd had a drink — we usually let kids over thirteen have a sip of wine at the dinner table, on special occasions. As a way to teach how to drink responsibly, to associate drinking with dinner and family and conversation. I apologize if we should have stepped in and prevented it."

He picked up the bottle and placed it across the table, away from Mariah.

It hadn't occurred to me that I was in the position to mind anything these adults did at all, and then I remembered, yes, I was the older sister, and an adult, too, at least officially. I had some kind of authority here.

"It's okay," I said. "In my family, people usually do their drinking alone in a dark room, so your idea is probably better."

I hadn't meant it as a joke, but Stefan leaned his head back and laughed so loudly he distracted Willow and Mariah from their conversation.

"Your sister is hilarious. Did you know that?"

Mariah nodded. Her face was red and her eyes glassy. "She's my favorite person in the world and she can always make me laugh."

I smiled, but Mariah's loopy look made me wonder how much she'd actually drunk. Seemed like more than a few sips. It was fine for us to drink together, but I didn't know she drank without me, too.

As dinner wound down, the kids made their way up to bed. Stefan went to tuck them in and Willow opened another bottle of wine for herself and brought us to her art room.

Mariah leaned on me, her eyes glassy.

"Go get a glass of water," I whispered in her ear, and she nodded, gliding out of the room. I felt the strange, unfamiliar sensation of frustration with Mariah. She was drunk, there was no

29

denying it. It'd seen her drunk before. And she'd lied to me about how much wine she'd had. But we were in an unfamiliar house, her employers' house, and I didn't want to embarrass her.

Willow watched her leave.

"We are so lucky to have her," Willow said, touching me on the shoulder and leaving it there, pulling me close.

"I get the sense that you girls are a little lonely out here. All on your own."

I shrugged. "We've got each other," I said. She nodded at me, encouraging more. "That's always been enough before," I told her. "I guess things are changing, though. We both have jobs, lives separate from each other during the day. It's different from how it used to be. We've always been best friends, too, not just sisters."

She squeezed my shoulder. I managed to gently twist myself from her grasp.

"That's sweet," she said. "I wish I'd had a sister who felt like a friend and made me feel at home. My own sister lives in some condo in Denver and complains about the traffic. I listen to her yammering on and on and sometimes I just turn up the volume on the cordless phone and leave it on the counter and go about my business, barely listening. I can't figure out what she wants me to say in response."

She shrugged, as if to get rid of the memory of her sister, and disconnected from me, gliding toward enormous canvases on the wall.

"I'm trying to paint more often. Painting is usually Stefan's area, at least, where he's been a real artist. I paint to pay the bills and save my art for other things, like these...dolls." She gestured toward a figure on the wall, a fabric creature that emerged from what looked like the beginning of a traditional tapestry but ended in a fragmentary, frayed collection of eyes and hands and feet.

"Lately I've been painting like mad, just locking myself in here for hours. I've been working on these things for so long that I can barely tell if they're any good anymore. What do you think?"

This was the kind of question I could answer. I'd never met a test I couldn't pass.

It helped that I loved the paintings immediately, and while I didn't know much about art, I'd learned how to please people: reflect them back to themselves with enthusiasm.

"I love that blue in the middle of the biggest one, that big pop of color." I'd read 'pop of color' in a fashion magazine and it sounded right. Willow smiled.

"I love that color, too," she said. "People think blue is about sadness but it's such a happy color. Peacock blue."

I nodded. "I also like how all the squiggly, unruly parts seem to be gathered up in the corner, like the blue forced them to the side."

Her eyes were alight again; I had interested her.

Mariah came back in and watched us talking about the paintings.

"They're beautiful," she said. "I don't understand them, though."

Willow glanced at me, her lips upturned. "No need to understand something beautiful. The need to understand it kills it."

I felt a wicked little pleasure that Mariah had gotten it wrong and I'd gotten it right.

But then, Willow reached out to pull Mariah next to her, and Mariah fell against her shoulder and melted into her body. I had never held Mariah that way, and I'd never seen her melt into anyone else that way, either, at least not in a decade or so. It was how children fell into their mothers when being comforted. It had been a long time since I'd seen that or felt it myself. I wished I could walk over to Willow and melt into her like that, too, but I couldn't figure out how, the motion was so foreign to me. You had to trust the person would hold you. You had to trust that they truly wanted you there. It seemed a risk not worth taking. I was on my way out anyway.

We wandered back out to the living room, where Stefan had opened up another glass of wine.

"I didn't know if you wanted a sip, too," he said, motioning a glass with just a couple of splashes of wine in it toward me. "And we'd love to have you over a bit longer if you can stay."

"Oh no," I said, reflexively, "we better get back." But Mariah said *yes* before I could stop her.

Stefan smiled at us both.

"Which is it?" He asked. "Stay or go?"

I looked at Mariah. "Please," she said. "Let's just stay a little longer."

I eyed the glass on the table. I would only live the first summer of my eighteenth year once. I picked up the glass and downed it, the little trickle of fluid warm in my mouth.

We came home late, giggling, tripping over our ridiculously long dresses. Stefan had called us ghosts, he said we were like *two angels gliding through the night*. After Mariah and I had secretly splashed the equivalent of a couple of cups of wine into our glasses, we'd gone out to the yard and ran around barefoot as Stefan played guitar and Willow watched us, laughing, joining in. As if we'd planned it, we all joined hands in a circle and spun and spun until we went too fast and flew apart, falling hard on the ground, dizzy from spinning and the wine. I took a hard knock against a gnarled maple and found myself on the ground, contemplating if I'd broken my shoulder, and a few moments later, wondering if I should give in to the subtle, steadily building desire to throw up. I stayed on my back for a full minute more until both feelings melted away. Mariah's hand appeared before my face and I took it. She lifted me up and we joined Stefan and Willow for a last song, singing still as we made our way across the yard, which reflected the moonlight on the little slivers of grass.

June, 1999

We woke late, long after the sun had thrown itself across our bodies. I was still wearing Maria's dress, now sticky and clinging, the sweat and salt and tang of alcohol emanating from me. I couldn't stand the tacky feel of my skin. My mouth was dry, so I rushed to the bathroom and put my head under the faucet. I could feel the alcohol inside of me, heating my body, coming through my pores, banging around in my forehead. As I slurped the water from the running faucet, my stomach protested, and I vomited into the toilet.

I wasn't sure how I had drank so much: I hadn't at any point had even a whole glass at once, but somehow the night had caught up with me.

I waited until my stomach settled again, took a quick shower to get the sick layer of the night off my skin and hair, then dressed in a loose t-shirt and stumbled down to find Mariah already eating breakfast, looking as sick as me, and Bobbie peeking over the edge of the local paper at us, noting our misery.

"Long night?" she asked.

I shrugged. "We were just over at the neighbors, where

Mariah works."

"I remember," she said. "I sent you along with some wine, if I remember correctly. It wasn't meant to be for you."

I nodded, then looked down at my food, feeling out how Bobbie would respond.

"How did you like them?" She asked.

"They seem nice. They really like Mariah."

Bobbie nodded. "They sure do," she said. "It's nice to have little children in the neighborhood again. It's mostly us old people in big, empty houses along this street. There haven't been children here since you two were girls. So you girls went out after, right? By the looks of you both you must have had quite a good time." Bobbie's mouth had gone thin and tight and I realized she was upset with us, not amused. Only our first week, and already we'd broken her trust.

Bobbie set down her paper and pursed her lips. "You know, I'm happy to give you two some freedom, but I need to know where you are when you do go somewhere. I have to keep you safe. I know you girls don't get out that much back home, but that's all the more reason to keep me in the loop in case you get in trouble."

Mariah and I exchanged a look. Mariah was fifteen, still, and I didn't want her to get sent back home with Mom because I couldn't keep a handle on her behavior. Truthfully, we'd been drinking secretly for years. Looking back, I don't know how we both avoided becoming alcoholics. I suppose we chose other vices.

"Don't worry," I said. "We stayed at their house. I was

with her the whole time. And Willow and Stefan were with us, too. I swear, we didn't run off with teenagers or do any illegal substances."

"And I don't even like that kind of thing, going out like that," Mariah said. "I'm not…wild."

"So how did you two end up hungover? They gave you alcohol?"

I paused, thinking of how to frame it in a way that wouldn't get Mariah or them in trouble.

"I let Mariah have a sip of wine — they didn't see until later on, after we'd both had a few…sips. They asked if we were allowed and we let them know you usually let us have a glass on holidays." I shrugged, ducking my head. "I figured since it was a special occasion it was like a holiday." This was weak, but I hoped it would at least put the heat back on me.

"So, they didn't stop you?"

I shook my head. "They asked me to check with you next time, to make sure it was okay. It all happened so fast, I should have thought it through better."

"Hmm," Bobbie said, regarding her coffee and not me.

"If it helps, they talked about how they believe in drinking responsibility. Like over dinner, over conversation, that kind of thing."

Bobbie glanced out the window, at the sleeping house across the lawn.

"I don't know how I feel about that," she said. I could see her thinking. "Well, maybe if your mother and I had learned that lesson as teenagers then things would have been different."

"I'm sorry," I said. "I shouldn't have assumed…"

She waved my apology away. "It's okay. It sounds like you pulled one over on them. They should have stopped you, but also, they seem like a bunch of hippies, so I can also imagine them thinking it was nothing."

"I really wasn't trying to fool anyone," I said, feeling a little indignant that she'd assume I was being deceitful with them, even as I was being deceitful to her. "I just figured it was okay, and then realized I forgot to check. I *was* looking out for Mariah, I promise." My mouth wobbled, and to my horror, I was close to tears with real emotion. It *was* my job to look out for her, and I hadn't.

Bobbie turned toward me and her mouth went soft. "I know you were. I've never doubted that. I remember when you were young. You were never *bad*, but you were independent. I knew if you disappeared that I'd find you somewhere together, probably curled up in bed reading a book or in the attic, playing with Cassandra's boxes of old dresses."

Mariah and I exchanged a glance and then turned back to Bobbie, wondering what would come next. She rarely spoke about Cassandra, not since she'd died. I waited for the moment where her face might fall or change, where she'd clam up and become her usual buttoned-up self, but it didn't fall. She was still smiling, looking past us through the window, where the lawn was illuminated, undifferentiated, just a fuzzy burst of sun and green.

"I remember those dresses," Mariah said, breaking the static. "She'd drag them out and get us out her portable closet on wheels with all those hangers wrapped in fabric."

I remembered, too. Those dresses were a dream, slippery and glittery and stiff and loose, dresses for every occasion or level of formality, cocktail dresses and summer dresses and woolen suit dresses you'd wear in an office.

"She never wore them herself. I wondered why, they were still beautiful and she clearly loved them."

Bobbie smiled. "She loved them, but they weren't her life anymore. She loved costume, loved the way clothes could tell a story. She was a dancer, did you girls know that? A lot of those clothes had been her performance clothes. She loved dancing, but it ruined her knees, so she moved on to swimming."

We hadn't known that. We hadn't known much of anything about her personal life.

Bobbie put down her newspaper. "I want to talk about her," she said. She nodded to herself, as if completing a conversation she was having in her head. She stood up and made her way into the living room, where she sat down on the couch and patted the seat next to her. "Come sit by me. It's time we talk about her, about all of it. It was a loss for you, too, and I never said anything about that."

"It's okay," I said, following her lead and taking a seat. "You don't have to talk about it if you don't want to."

Her sudden desire to talk about Cassandra had saved me from more questions, but I wasn't sure *I* wanted to talk about her. I didn't know what I'd do if Bobbie fell apart in front of us. I liked having an adult in the house who didn't cry near-daily.

Bobbie shook her head. "It's not okay that we haven't

talked about it. It's not okay because she was part of your lives. You must have been hurting, too. You loved her, and she loved you. And I know you mother...your mother loves you, but it's hard for her. She doesn't always, isn't always able..."

I nodded. "I understand." I didn't want her to have to say it. Our mother was a drunk who couldn't be there for us. She disappointed us and she disappointed herself.

"Cassandra would talk about you both, even toward the end. She wanted to know that you were going to be okay. She saw what was happening with your mom, even before I did, that she was starting to slip. I was distracted with Cassandra and keeping her alive, but I see now that Cassandra knew she wasn't going to make it, early on she knew. I don't mean in some supernatural way, she had just fully accepted what the doctor said — the chances were slim. She asked me to make sure you both were safe, to intervene if things got too bad." Bobbie took my hand and then reached out for Mariah's as well. "I think that I've let you both down."

I shook my head. "We're okay, Bobbie."

"Cleo isn't okay, though, is she?"

I hesitated for a moment. "No."

She nodded. "Cassandra warned me. She told me that at some point, I would have to take you both in because your mother wouldn't be able to care for you anymore. She made me promise."

Because Mom's decline had followed so swiftly after Cassandra's death, and because our family's habit was to smooth things over and keep things secret, I had not really thought much about my own grief over Cassandra, a woman I'd known since I was a child. Even before she moved in with Bobbie, she'd been around, *Bobbie's friend*, picking us up from school if Mom forgot, as she often did before we could walk home ourselves. She'd take us to get some ice cream or a paper bag full of candy from the corner store, where you could fill it up to the brim for just three dollars. I'd pick atomic fireballs and chocolate. Mariah liked dusty, hard candies, like wafers and candy necklaces. Cassandra had helped me and Mariah learn to ride a bike because Mom didn't like the sunshine, it triggered her migraines, and the sidewalks near our apartment were broken and ended abruptly, leading to a two-lane road with a narrow shoulder. Mariah had once rolled her tricycle right off the edge and into rush hour traffic. Cassandra had been there, thank God, and had dragged her back moments before a truck roared by. *We're gonna practice at Bobbie's from now on*, she said that day, holding our hands tight as she marched us home.

Everything about her had been easy and elegant and matter-of-fact. She wore soft sweaters and jeans or simple dresses in rich, heavy fabrics, dresses that made her athletic body a long, lean line of color or pattern. Her death had seemed unreal: I'd seen her only a week before her death, in a hospital bed, bald, but still talking, still asking me about school and my plans for the future. She had remained composed and even cheerful as she asked me about a future she wasn't going to live to see. We understood she had cancer, but she had never seemed *sick* and certainly not dying. We'd known that Cassandra had cancer for so long that I was lulled into believing that she was going to be okay. Her treatment had made her hair fall out, but she'd covered it up with colorful scarves and showed up to holidays and school events anyway, as she always did. She never talked about it, and we didn't, either, even as she grew thinner and slower in those last months.

I surprised myself by beginning to cry. Of course Cassandra had loved us, I had never doubted that. But I had never fully recognized it, either. Her role in our lives as Bobbie's *friend*, then something like her *wife*, though they never made it exactly clear what they were to each other, and the gradual, then sudden way that she died, had obscured something obvious. I had not known how to mourn for her because I didn't know how to say exactly who she was to me.

"She was the best person I'd ever met," Bobbie said. "She had this gift for making the world more comfortable. She wanted this house to be somewhere you girls could come and be happy, where everything else would fall away. She made the garden something magical and the house this big, airy space. I've let it all go to shit since she's been gone. Crowded the upstairs rooms with boxes. Made it a mess."

Bobbie looked around the room, gesturing at the sink full of dishes, the spiderwebs in the corners, and out the window, where the boundaries of Cassandra's flower garden were unclear in the general overgrown, weedy mess, the fences long knocked over. Compared to back home, it was spotless, but I understood what she meant in comparison to how it had been before. Cassandra had been firmly anchored in the world, the environment, so without her, Bobbie had retreated. She had used the same set of cups and dishes for years, nearly, just washing the same ones over and over again, reducing every necessary thing down to the basics. Which meant she'd let so many small things go.

"She'd be ashamed of me if she could see it the way it looks right now. We used to lie in bed upstairs and look out the big window over the yard and admire the flowers, the grass, this place we'd made new together. I just shut the curtains nowadays."

"When I grew up here with your mother, it was an unhappy place — always cold, the pipes old and leaking, our mom in the kitchen making dinner miserably, as though she didn't want to be there: and she didn't, who could blame her? Our dad would come home drunk around seven, early enough to eat and kiss us goodnight before they'd start to argue and we had to put ourselves to bed. Cassandra swept all of that away. She made this place *ours*."

Bobbie paused her monologue to look down at her hands, where she was playing with the ring that I realized, in that moment, had probably been from Cassandra.

"We can do the dishes," I offered, feeling like I should contribute something. "We can help clean things up like they used to be."

Mariah nodded. "I could, too. I could do the floors, or dust all the surfaces." She gestured up at the ceiling fan blades, which were thick with dirt which flung down in strings whenever we switched it on.

Bobbie nodded. "It's not ever going to be the same, but you're right that we could make some changes around here. She's gone, but I'm still here, right? She wouldn't want me to Grey Gardens the place without her."

I felt ashamed that I hadn't thought to do much more than

pile my dishes in the sink and halfheartedly dry them when Mariah or Bobbie got around to the pile. We treated the house like a hotel. That's how it worked back home. Our house was dark, with bulbs burnt out in most rooms, hiding the piles of magazines and laundry and dusty picture frames. I had stopped caring that much when I was there. I cleaned only what absolutely had to be done in order to have a dish for a meal or a cup for coffee in the morning. I had brought that feeling of carelessness along with me without even noticing it.

"We can fix the garden, too," Mariah said. "That can be our biggest job while we're here. We shouldn't just stay without helping you."

Bobbie shook her head. "I appreciate it, and I'd love your help, but all of this wasn't meant to be your job," she said. "It was meant to be *for* you. Cassandra wanted you to have a safe place to come to."

"We can pull the weeds," I said. "We can dust the corners. We can do the dishes. We're almost adults now. Maybe we should be the ones to make things beautiful for you."

Bobbie smiled. "Would you know a weed from a plant that belongs there?"

"I'll pull the weeds after you show me which ones are weeds."

We laughed together at how little we knew about what a good growing thing is versus one that will choke the life out of a garden. The sun was hot on my face. I remember thinking that I would never forget this moment, me and Mariah and Bobbie, planning to restore the house, to honor Cassandra. It almost felt as though she were here, maybe in the pool of sunshine that fell between us. The sun warmed the room so much Mariah shrugged off her dressing gown, a purple, floral thing that she'd stolen from Mom before we left home, and it fell to the floor in a puddle of heat.

After we made practical plans, Bobbie looked faraway again. "I loved Cassandra and I was lucky to know her. I wish I'd had her longer. I wish we hadn't been so devoted to not talking about personal things, to never hugging or kissing around you. I worry sometimes you girls didn't know what she meant to me or thought we were hiding."

I shook my head. "I knew you loved each other."

Bobbie nodded. "Good."

"I hope you can know what it's like to find a person who makes your life better the way Cassandra made my life better."

Mariah and I nodded, but we didn't really understand. In my own head, I imagined a person who could *make me happy*, a person who could lift my mood, who would whisk me away from wherever I was and bring me to some happier future. It took me a long time to realize this was the wrong way to think about love.

Maybe Mariah could see that desire for escape on my face that day, that I held onto some hope that I could get *away*. More likely, none of us fully knew what was happening then, even in our own minds. We wiped away our tears and made another pot of coffee and went on with our lives.

March, 2016

When I last heard from Mariah, she had called me from an unknown number. I was pregnant, far along enough to tell people without feeling nervous but still early enough that my pregnant body was a mystery to me, full of new complaints and strange sensations. She congratulated me, and it felt genuine. I heard the same shuffling and voices in the background as always, but for the first time in a long time, I could tell I had interested her. So I took the opportunity to pull her closer to me.

"I can't wait for you to meet him. Or her." I said. We had decided not to learn the sex or do any kind of gender reveal. Colin's family had protested but ultimately relented. My family was almost nonexistent, except Bobbie, who thought it was ridiculous and vulgar to celebrate a baby's genitals anyway.

"Oh Chelsea," she said, with real warmth. "You'll be a good mother. How does Colin feel about the news?"

I turned to look at him where he sat in the living room, trying to read a book while also watching baseball. He felt my eyes on him and waved.

"He's happy. He's always wanted kids. It was hard for me

to understand that when we first got together. I've always felt so uncertain about it."

This was not usually the kind of information I'd offer in casual conversation, even with Mariah. Well, truthfully, particularly with Mariah.

When I told Colin how difficult it was to talk to my sister, how much history had come between us, he advised that I try some *honesty*.

"Tell her something that shows your vulnerability. I know that sounds like a bad idea, but it's like when a dog rolls over to show you its stomach. You showing vulnerability means you think she's safe. It shows trust."

Colin is a professional mediator. Every day, he sits between two people who cannot figure out how to speak to each other and diffuses the tension in the air. He feels confident that anyone can speak to anyone else, if only they both come with open hands, with humility and a willingness to listen to the other.

It's a sweet idea, but I don't believe it. More accurately, I don't believe it for myself. Sometimes people use your vulnerability against you. Sometimes people see you coming to them with open hands and want to fill those hands with their own problems. Sometimes you roll over and show your stomach and they kick you right in the soft spot.

I think his mediation works because *he's* the person between them. His basic decency, his stubborn unwillingness to believe that some things are just broken, it works like a magic spell, at least in the minutes when he's between these two angry people, his hands on the table, his face open and warm. Plus, the people who walk into his office either want to make things work or have to by orders of some outside pressure, like courts or kids or assets, so it makes sense they eventually give in and compromise. Still, I wanted to believe what he believes, that people want what's best for each other, that they want to compromise.

I plunged forward with an attempt at honesty in my usual, awkward way. I was aware of Colin in the next room, listening. At least nobody could say I hadn't tried.

"Sometimes I'm scared to have this baby, Mariah. I think about Mom and how I never saw her happy, you know? I think about our father, who I don't remember and you barely met, how he just disappeared and never came back. What if I'm like them? What if I'm unhappy and I give that unhappiness to my kid, like a disease?"

"You've gotta stop thinking like this," Mariah said. "I know it feels like you can't do it because you haven't had an example, but maybe that's the example — give the kid everything we needed but didn't get. Don't do what they did."

I laughed. "Okay, so I gotta not leave and not drink myself to death. It's a low bar, but I think I can do it."

From the living room, Colin looked up. I waved his concerned look away and laughed again, louder, to let Mariah know I was simply joking, just whistling in the dark.

She didn't laugh with me. "You've got to find a way to heal these old wounds, Chelsea. What happened to Mom wasn't funny. Our father was a sad person, incapable of being a parent to us. It's all just sad."

I changed the subject. I didn't like it when she took this

tone with me, of gentle knowing, as if she were the sister who had her life together and I was just a fuckup. We were both fuckups.

"Well, where are you living now?" I asked.

"For over a year I've been staying with a group called The Family Circle. It's an intentional community. We practice self-sufficiency, we take care of each other, all take turns cooking meals and watching the kids. It's pretty magical. We're up in the Adirondacks, on a sprawling old farm, lots of little living quarters, a huge garden."

"That sounds great," I said. What I was really thinking was that The Family Circle sounded culty as hell and that we lived in upstate New York, too, and she had not even attempted to come visit. Colin's family had sold us a house long kept in the family, thirty minutes from his work in a nearby decent-sized city, five minutes from a scenic little art town, the kind of place that's run on summer people's city money and old fashioned shops, which the locals frequented because frankly, it was easier to spend twenty more dollars for groceries than drive all the way into a place with some big-box store. It was more than that, too — we wanted to keep the place alive. Colin's family lived in scattered little hamlets throughout the state, all devoted townies. I had grown up hating my own poverty, my shitty town, its shabby history of being adjacent to larger, bigger places and events, but Colin didn't feel that way about where he came from. He genuinely believed his town was a *good place*. I remember once, at a family gathering, listening to his family talking about the town with glowing, loving nostalgia and realizing that I didn't feel like that about any place. Every place had the potential to fall apart, every place fell short. But his family had money, so maybe having money means you can make any place a good place.

She'd lived nearby and had never tried to see me. This fact rose up as she talked to me about something she was learning, about the plants she was tending, until again, I felt forced to use the most blunt instrument I had. I'd try out *honesty and vulnerability* again.

"I'd love to see you, Mariah. I remember when we'd talk about having kids together, about living close to each other, our kids being friends the way we were friends. Now that you're close, maybe we could do that. Be near each other again." I paused, not sure how to put what I really wanted to say. "We could talk, really talk, about what happened. If that would help."

I picked at a tear in the wallpaper as I waited for her response. The old farmhouse was covered in wallpaper, yellowing pink roses in the kitchen and huge sprays of violets in the living room, so many florals that walking downstairs in the bright light of morning sometimes felt like falling into a garden. I leaned my weight back and forth against two creaky floorboards, listening for the slight whine of pressure. It made me think of Bobbie's house, that constant racket beneath my feet and everywhere when the wind kicked up, when the weather grew dramatically colder or hotter and I could feel the wood and nails and plaster expanding or contracting. .

"Chelsea, I don't think I'm ever going to have kids." It was her turn to pivot and ignore, seizing on the most obvious part of what I'd said.

"That's okay," I said, starting to feel the old panic when I felt Mariah turn away from me. "I am. I am, and I want you here. We live over here in the woods, too, you know? We could be each other's community."

I had shifted to begging her now, my voice rising. I knew I'd already lost her but I didn't know how to stop.

"When I can come, I'll come, but right now, the organization needs me."

"I need you," I said. Colin caught my eye and pointed to himself, asking if I needed his help — to hold his hand, to have him sit near me as I cried, as he had so many other times. I shook my head. I would do this on my own. "I miss being close to you and I don't want to do this alone."

There, I said it. I didn't want to do this alone. I didn't even know how I felt about *this* — family, children, even marriage, though I'd been married for two years at this point. I was still surprised every time I wrote my new last name. I had never imagined myself as somebody's wife, as somebody's mother. This was a soft, strange role that I didn't understand how to inhabit.

"You won't be alone. You'll have Colin. I'm sure that Bobbie will come up, too."

I could feel my anger building. She was avoiding my question. Worse, she wouldn't say what I needed to hear.

"I don't want Colin," I shouted, feeling all the helplessness and frustration pour out of me. "I want you. I want things to be the way they used to be. I don't want to fucking beg you to be my sister."

I was turned away from him, but I could hear Colin stand up and walk upstairs. The ancient, creaking boards gave everything away, and Colin had a heavy step. Maybe I'd hurt him, as I often did when my anger exploded.

"You are going to be a wonderful mother," Mariah said, her voice thin, unconvincing. "I think, if you want it to be, this can be the thing that connects you to something deeper in yourself, that will help heal all of these old wounds, help fix all the guilt that holds you back."

All of the fire from my anger was gone. I was exhausted from wanting what didn't seem to exist anymore.

"I don't have guilt, Mariah. I just love you and miss you is all."

"I have a lot of love, too," Mariah said. "And I have faith that you know the kind of mother you need to be. I'll visit as soon as I can."

I have a lot of love, too. Not *I love you, too.* She couldn't even say it as a formality.

She hung up gently with a rushed, soft goodbye that didn't give me time to respond.

When I ended the call, I looked at what I'd done to the wall — I'd torn an enormous strip of paper away, revealing a lilac-colored paint beneath.

I leaned against the wall, trying hard to keep down my breakfast. I was feeling the spasmodic flutterings of growth inside me. It felt exactly like I imagined it would feel to swallow a small, clawed animal, one that wanted out. I made my way to the staircase to visit the bathroom and throw up before I apologized to Colin.

July 1999

The talk with Bobbie changed things at the house. We took ownership of our rooms and put our dresses up on hangers instead of keeping them in wrinkled piles on the floor. We gathered up our stained coffee cups and soaked the brown spots out. In the garden, Bobbie pointed out the weeds from the flowers and showed us how to pull them out at the root to make room for the perennials that would take their place next spring.

"It's a lost cause this summer," she told us, "but by next year, it'll be blooming again."

We all had a beach day. Mariah and I wore two of Cassandra's old bathing suits, both busty with foam padding and a nude, tummy control panel at the stomach. We let the cold, crashing waves suck us under water and then spit us up and out again. A couple of times, I felt myself being thrown off of my feet and dragged underwater, but I caught myself and rose back up, gasping.

Mariah liked the feeling of being taken under, liked the way she could muscle her way out of it.

"It's like being on a rollercoaster," she said as we sat on the beach in the sun, eating cheese and crackers and listening to a little shower radio we'd found in the attic. "Except the risk is real, which makes it even more exciting."

I shook my head. "I don't need to mix fun and risk."

Bobbie agreed. "Life will give you enough real ways to get close to death; you don't have to chase it." She'd watched us fighting the water from the shore, burying her face in a newspaper when we went too far out.

"Don't say I didn't warn you," she shouted to Mariah after the third time she was dragged under and I had to help her from being swept out into the open water.

At work, I'd gotten closer to Jackson, who wanted to be a writer but had to save money to support himself the first year of school. He'd applied for a bachelor's degree in creative writing at the state college, an hour away, but he'd had to defer his half scholarship because his parents wouldn't pay the rest of the balance.

"Bummer," I said. I was in his car, smoking weed after work. It had become our ritual, but so far, Jackson hadn't touched me, hadn't even tried to, and I was beginning to feel confused and irritated by his inconsistent intimacy — he told me things you'd only tell a close friend, but we weren't really friends. He had told me about his parents, working-class people who had cleaned hotel rooms and drove taxis and done all the various kinds of work you could do in a vacation town. We had this in common, but I didn't tell him. I simply nodded sympathetically and let him talk. He told me about how they hadn't understood him, how they had told him he needed a plan B.

"Like a plan B ever worked for them," he said.

I nodded and smoked his weed and listened to the music he played on the car radio, the speaker on my side busted and buzzing at every bass note, but nothing else happened. He had asked me about myself, briefly, but I kept it short and skeletal, giving just enough of a hint of family problems to keep me interesting, but not too many so I wouldn't scare him away.

But he'd never tried to kiss me. I started to take it personally. He would say things about liking hanging around with me, even went so far as to invite me to a movie, but as much as I tried to get my face close to his, to make myself available, he didn't take the bait. I refused the movie, an action thing that seemed so noisy and incoherent I feared it would give me a migraine and put me in a bad mood.

It felt good to refuse him something, to act like I didn't want to be near him, but he just shrugged and went back to washing the dishes. It was strange to want somebody, not something I enjoyed feeling. It was more like an addiction than a joy, and I had already decided that I wouldn't become addicted to anything. After a while, I wasn't sure if I wanted him because I was genuinely attracted to him or because he hadn't made any move toward me. I think back on myself then and feel such an acute sadness that I had already started to confuse being seen with being wanted, desire with being desired.

When I wasn't working, I'd go over to Stefan and Willow's house and hang out with Mariah while she watched the kids. They didn't require much watching, really — they did as they pleased most of the day, asking only for help setting up art projects or making sandwiches or turning on the TV to watch one of the hundreds of VHS tapes the family had stacked all around the living room in battered cases. Some were the usual kid stuff, but a lot of strange films, too — *Cabaret,* with Liza Minella and Joel Grey belting out depressive songs on a grimy, dark stage during the waning years of the Weimar Republic, or *Plague Dogs,* an animated film about animals escaped from a medical testing facility trying to figure out how to live in the wild. I haven't seen that second film since, but I can still remember a terrier with a shaved skull talking about the flies buzzing in his brain after a surgery. Somehow, this grim fare paired with *The Little Mermaid* and *Wishbone,* and nobody seemed to mind or find it strange.

Most of the time, the kids were outdoors making up their own games or reading, so Mariah and I either sat in the shade and watched them or sat at the kitchen window drinking cup after cup of coffee or sometimes cold white wine orange slices garnishing our wine glasses along the top. Willow and Stefan didn't venture out much during the day — they stayed locked up in their rooms, sleeping or making art, sometimes emerging for food or coffee, which Mariah kept brewed all day, making a fresh pot before she left every night.

I loved their house. It was a friendly shambles that would have slid into filthy territory without Mariah. With Mariah to tidy up throughout the day, though, it was pleasant, piles of books and faint smell of paint and dog hair on the couch and dust in the air, but also the smell of oranges and flowers and window cleaner.

Where Bobbie's house was spare, theirs was filled with little objects, things lodged between the couch cushions and under the coffee table, with children's drawings on the refrigerator and a new junk drawer, already overflowing.

Once, Stefan emerged from his art room, bleary-eyed, shirtless, and saw us both in the kitchen, on our fourth cup of coffee. We were giggling, though I was shaky and sick to my stomach, too. Being at Willow and Stefan's encouraged my burgeoning habit of ignoring my body on purpose. I hadn't eaten anything and could feel my stomach churning, but instead I kept downing coffee.

"What time is it?" he asked.

"Two," Mariah answered. He nodded, but didn't seem to hear or care about the answer. He poured a cup of coffee and drank it while looking at us.

"You're both like a dream," he said. He walked over, standing close to me, and placed his hand on my head. The pressure there felt comforting, felt natural, fatherly even. He removed his hand and walked back to the room after getting a glass of water. I wanted him to stay but was also relieved when he left — he carried a tension lately, or maybe I did when around him.

"Does he walk around like that all the time?" I didn't like that he felt comfortable enough to be with us while half-naked. I also didn't want to seem like a prude.

Mariah shrugged. "It's no big deal. They both walk around however they want."

"However they want?"

She shrugged again, avoiding. "Chelsea, don't be weird about it." She met my eyes. "I know you hate people seeing your body, but not everyone is like that."

I looked at her, waiting for her to soften it somehow, but she continued drinking her cup of coffee. She'd never compared me negatively with anyone else before.

I was very, very high the night Jackson finally kissed me, just a couple of days after Mariah implied I was afraid to show my body, that I was a *prude*, the opposite of an adult woman looking for an adult relationship. I usually took one or two puffs and then waved the joint away, not wanting to be wobbly on my way back home, but that night, I felt reckless and lonely, still smarting from what Mariah had said, feeling funny about Stefan. I kept accepting the joint until it burned down to my fingers and I had to shove them into an old soda cup he had in his cup holder to keep a blister from rising.

The world felt fuzzy. My peripheral vision twitched, making me think people were at the windows, waving us to open them. *Somebody's watching us*, I thought. I was very aware of my hand on Jackson's knee. I caught the frequency of his voice. He was talking about himself again, about a novel he was reading that was full of annotations and written only in second person.

"What's it about?" I asked him.

He shrugged. "It's more about the way it's written than a plot or anything, you know. The characters all have the same name, so it's hard to even know what's going on."

Something he'd said before floated back to me as I stared

up at the ceiling.

"Second person," I repeated. "Like all in letters to somebody?"

"No," he said, "that's eipisto...epistomo...epi-something. This is like, saying *you* when you mean *I*."

"Huh," I said, trying to remain interested, to keep it all together.

"So the characters all have the same name," I said. "Maybe they're all the same person." I thought maybe if I was interested enough this conversation could lead me straight through to being sober again, but it didn't seem to be working.

My brain was buzzing, full of associations that in the moment, seemed surprising and new. As I moved my hand up Jackson's leg, I thought about Mariah's job, about Willow and Stefan and how much they loved her, how free they were with their affection, at least compared to me. Willow had held my hand without worrying if her hand was sweaty or if I might not want to hold it, she seemed to believe that no matter the status of her hand, she was worthy of having it held. Stefan had hugged me tight when we left that first night, and since then, I'd gotten tight hugs from them every time we crossed paths. They knew it was important to be touched, to feel cared for.

It wasn't bad to need to be touched, was it? It wasn't bad to want something simple. It was okay that I was interested in Stefan, naturally. He was old enough to be my father, but he wasn't my father and I was eighteen. I was allowed to desire just like anyone else.

And then, it was happening: James kissed me, and then just

as quickly pulled away.

"I have a girlfriend," he blurted. "She works at Dunkin Donuts in the next town over."

I nodded, ready to seem agreeable, even as something warm and hopeful shriveled up inside me. I also wanted to laugh out loud, imagining his girlfriend behind the Dunkin Donuts counter, serving crullers and syrupy, khaki-colored coffee, while we sat here high as hell, trying to grasp a simple conversation.

"Hey, that's cool," I said. "I'm not trying to get in the way of that. I can get out of here if you need me to."

I'd been wrong, like always. I'd been wrong before about people showing their affection. Once, at one of the rare parties I'd gone to in high school, I drank too much too quickly and ended up stuck to a couch for most of the party, trying to keep myself from throwing up. While I was parked there, a particularly desirable football player who also happened to be smart had talked to me for five minutes straight, a rare thing for me, a girl who'd spent most of high school avoiding anybody's notice and standing in the background of yearbook group pictures, my face usually obscured by somebody else's head.

He was telling me about something happening at school, something he was part of that I wasn't, so I simply nodded, and then he glanced toward the door and said "Let's get out of here and smoke some weed."

I froze up. "Oh," I said. "I don't smoke."

The football player looked down at me, confused, and then laughed. Behind me, more laughter. I turned and saw a girl so beautiful, so far beyond me in grace and charm and any other rubric by which you might judge somebody that it seemed ridiculous we were the same species. He'd been talking to her the whole time, and in the dim room and contacts from years ago, when I'd last had a checkup, I'd mistaken his glance over my head as being directed at me.

So it had happened again, me thinking I meant more to somebody than I really did.

I pulled away and started to feel around among the trash on his floorboard to find my purse. He watched me, seemingly perplexed, and then grabbed my arm. "You don't understand," he said. "I don't want you to go. I like talking to you."

He looked at me, the word *talking* taking on some strange new meaning.

"I like talking to you, too."

"That's awesome," he said. Nodding to himself. "I don't get to see her much, but it's nice to have somebody to...talk to sometimes, when I can't see her, you know. I bet you feel the same way, too. Lonely like that, for somebody to talk to."

We both laughed. I don't know why he laughed, but I laughed because words no longer meant what they usually meant and I felt foolish and embarrassed and no other noise could incorporate all those feelings. I laughed because of course I was lonely, only I wasn't even lonely for somebody, like he was, I was lonely as a habit, as a general way of being. I laughed and laughed, struck by the silliness of language and my own life, so bereft of connection that this guy with a girlfriend was the closest thing I had to love. He laughed, too. I was still very, very high. He moved toward me again and I did not protest.

I got home late that night. As predicted, the bike ride had been terrifying and wobbly, though I sobered up halfway through, just in time to swerve out of the way of a driver who had drifted past the white line and into the bike lane.

We'd had sex, though we'd barely taken our clothes off. It had been quick and efficient and felt like nothing but warmth and friction. We slid our work pants down, and then back up again, never having to remove our shoes. I smelled fish in his hair, as he probably did in mine. High as I was, my brain was preoccupied the entire time with how little I was feeling. Did I even like kissing? The act seemed newly alien as I thought about the mechanics, about how private the mouth is. Strange that I was allowing another person into all of these private cavities.

Afterwards, he'd whispered *Thanks, that was fun* and then asked me if I wanted a ride home. I didn't want to ride my bike but I also wanted to immediately be as far from him as possible. A shame was starting to creep up, a layer on top of my paranoia, and suddenly I wondered if his girlfriend might know what we'd just done by some supernatural means, some intuition that I didn't have. I imagined her in Dunkin Donuts, hit with the knowledge as she wrapped up a stale, cherry-filled donut for some drunk customer.

At home, I took a hot shower and threw my clothes in the laundry. Bobbie was in bed, snoring gently — I checked on her and could see her pale face above the blankets, bluish in the moonlight from her window. She didn't have a curtain because she liked being awakened by natural light every morning, no matter the time.

Mariah wasn't home. She'd spent the night next door because Willow and Stefan were out on a date and they didn't expect to be back until well after one AM. I looked through our window and saw the living room light was on, a car in the driveway. They'd come back early.

Maybe she'll come home, I thought, hoping she would walk through the door any moment. I wouldn't tell her everything that had happened, not yet, but I needed help with this feeling of shame and loneliness that had hit me like a truck.

I got in bed, promising myself that I'd stay awake until she returned, but I fell asleep with my work clothes still on. When I woke in the morning, my makeup from the night before had deposited itself on my pillowcase and Mariah's bed was still made. She hadn't come home at all.

That morning, I scrubbed the makeup off my face and looked hard in the mirror — I looked old, blue circles under my eyes. My lips were dry and cracked and I couldn't get enough water. When I made it down to the kitchen Mariah was eating cereal, looking as fresh and lovely as ever.

"Why didn't you come back?" I asked. "I saw their car in the driveway when I got in at eleven. I wanted to tell you about my night."

Mariah put her finger to her lips as Bobbie entered the room in a blue, silken robe, something I'd never seen on her before. One of Cassandra's robes, probably. She seemed breezy and light, more awake than she'd been in a long time. Usually, she was up long before us, so she'd either been in her room or had slept in.

Mariah and I watched her sit down at the table and unfold her paper. She turned to Mariah.

"You were out late last night," she said. "I heard you coming in this morning."

"I did an overnight next door," Mariah said. "I told you about it."

"But they came back early, didn't they? Their car woke me up around eleven."

Not much got past Bobbie, that's what I thought then. I imagine that's what she thought about herself, too. We both imagined we were keeping Mariah safe, keeping tabs on things.

Mariah shrugged. "I was asleep on the couch by then," she said. "I guess they didn't want to wake me."

I remembered the light on in the living room. I didn't imagine Mariah, a girl who needed a fan and a mask to sleep, could have fallen asleep before eleven PM on a couch, especially not with lights on. She was the kind of person who needed a whole ritual before bed and a certain feel of sheets before she could even close her eyes.

I didn't say anything. Bobbie nodded and seemed to let it pass.

"How was *your* night?" Bobbie asked me.

I didn't want to talk about my night. "It was fine, just hung out with a friend for a while then headed home."

Bobbie looked back and forth between us at the table.

"Both of you look like you're hiding something," she said.

Mariah and I waited, saying nothing. We'd learned this

trick back home. Mom would start to rage about something, usually something imaginary or exaggerated, and often we could just wait her out if we didn't respond. She'd fizzle out or take her anger out on something else. Bobbie wasn't so easy to distract, though.

She looked back and forth between us, long enough to make it uncomfortable, but we didn't budge.

"I suppose you're allowed to keep your secrets," she said, finally. "But at least tell each other, okay?"

We nodded obediently and cleared the dishes. I volunteered to wash and Mariah to dry.

Bobbie took the paper away to her bedroom, where she'd stay for a while before work. We listened for her steps on the stairs, waiting until they gradually faded away.

Mariah turned to me as soon as we heard the door shut.

"What were you up to last night?" She asked, grinning. "Did you see Jackson?"

His name released all the tears I'd been holding back since the night before.

Mariah pulled me over to the couch, where she cradled my head against her shoulder.

"That bad?"

I nodded, trying to catch my breath.

"I was waiting to talk to you last night," I said. "You didn't come. I didn't have anyone else to talk to."

Mariah sighed and tried to run her hand through my tangled hair.

"Chelsea, your hair is a mess and you smell like weed and sweat. What happened? Did he do something? "

I shook my head. "I mean, he was an asshole, but not like that. He didn't do anything. Well, I mean we both did something. And I wish we hadn't."

"I'm sorry," she said. I rested against her and listened to her breathing, the small sounds inside her chest, until I stopped crying.

"It went wrong," I said. "It wasn't fun. I feel like shit."

"I thought he was just an experiment," she said. "You can't mess up an experiment. Isn't that what you always say, that anything that happens is experience?"

I closed my eyes. "I feel stupid. He has a girlfriend."

"Chelsea," she said, "Don't beat yourself up."

"I was shitty to another person and I can't fix it."

Mariah made a clicking noise, as our mother had when we were young and fighting with each other.

"You made a mistake," she said. "A mistake that lots of people have made. A mistake that he made, too. It wasn't just you. And this isn't the end of the world."

Mariah brushed my hair with her fingers until I fell asleep on the couch. When I woke up, the sun was slanting directly into my face, and the sink was empty, the dishes stacked neatly in the cabinet. I closed my eyes again and fell back asleep.

That day, I could have asked her about why she didn't come home. I could have asked her about her night. Maybe she would have told me something that would have stopped the whole thing right there. It's probably ridiculous to imagine I had that much power, but this is the moment I go back to, among them all and everything that happened later. She still loved me then. Maybe I could have stopped it all.

April, 2006

Our mother died a year before Mariah began to truly remove herself from my life. Her death had been long, but also a surprise. She had hung on for years at a low level of functioning, complaining of ailments that blurred into a vast constellation of complaints that we couldn't hear as real anymore. In the months after she died, we sold her house and used most of the money to pay the credit card debt we'd racked up to cremate her and hold a scant funeral, just for us and Aunt Bobbie and a few scattered cousins. We wore a tiny ball of her ashes inside of matching necklaces, blown glass globes that held a swirl of what appeared to be little black stars. The rest, we scattered in the ocean just a few blocks from Bobbie's house. We didn't know what else to do with the cremains. The idea of keeping her in the house seemed morbid, and neither of us had a permanent residence anyway.

Bobbie said she had once loved the sea, though by the time she became a parent she could barely stand being outside, the sun too bright, the noises too loud. So we had scattered her there, in a place she'd loved when she was still a girl, and full of promise.

I remembered feeling this hollow sadness as we threw what

was left of my mother into the waves. I didn't miss her, at least not the way she was before she died. She'd been so altered for so long that I hardly remembered the mother who had gathered us up in her lap to brush our hair before bed, and I had stopped longing for that mother, longing being more painful than forgetting. Before we sold the house, we had to clean out her room, which had become a nest filled with magazines and trash and empty bottles, some filled with urine, from those last months when even shuffling to the bathroom was more than she could take. It had gotten so bad that most things in the room were unsalvageable, boxes full of photographs and baby clothes, all of our childhood school pictures and holiday snapshots turned to rot, our faces warped and moldy.

Mariah and I had spent days together scraping away layers of newspaper that had been cemented to the floors, mopping up sticky stuff that used to be liquid. We talked then, almost like the old days. Mariah was about to go to Zurich for her Jungian dreamwork degree. She told me, with excitement, about how she wanted to understand her shadow. I felt quite acquainted with my shadows already and had no desire to know them better, but I was happy for her. After we cleaned up the house, we stayed with Bobbie for a couple of days, sinking into a normalcy that had felt so warm and inviting that even at the time, as it was happening, I mourned the fact that soon, I'd lose it.

"You girls didn't get to know her the way she was, before life beat her down," Bobbie told us as we drank wine and looked at old photographs she'd unearthed from boxes that had been sitting up in the attic all this time. Bobbie's pictures had not been ruined, so we had something to look at when we tried to remember our mother as whole and happy, not the skeletal mess she'd been when her home-health nurse found her unconscious on the floor or when she'd slipped away later that week at the hospital with Bobbie at her side. Neither of us had been able to come. I had not even considered coming, imagining she'd just passed out drunk again and that this would be like every other time she'd been hospitalized in the last couple of years, yet another false alarm for a woman who seemed to want to die but couldn't quite commit to it.

"Look at you girls," she said, pointing to a series of Polaroids my mother had taken when we were both toddlers. She'd dressed us for Easter in those early days, a gesture toward her childhood Catholicism. "When your father left, she threw herself into you two. As much as it changed later, I hope you can remember some of those early days and how devoted she was to you."

Sometimes I could remember. I was able to hold the sadness of the end of her life along with the way it was in those early years, that closed world she'd created for us that felt comfortably inaccessible to anyone else. I have longed for that for the rest of my life, a relationship that's like a rocketship you crawl into together, the turbulence only bringing you closer. I now recognize something wrong with this way of thinking about family, about the world around us as being equivalent to the depths of space. I used to think exclusivity was love. This was partly why Mariah's relationship with Stefan and Willow had started to get to me, why it felt like a threat, like something impossible to enter but also exactly what I thought love should look like.

When we went together to scatter the cremains, I held the box with both hands, terrified I would trip and dump it on the ground. It was heavier than I imagined it would be, having had no direct experience before with death except Cassandra, and even then I'd been kept from the details. I had not even seen her in the casket. Mom being estranged from most of her own family and not knowing my father's family had the benefit of insulating me from death, though I supposed in the long run it was a downside. I had little practice at loss, not even dead pets to mourn.

Bobbie had found us an isolated strip of shore for the ashes. It was tangled with weeds and shrubs, the drop-off too severe for swimming, water too shallow for diving. I had brought something to scoop them out with, not wanting to touch the cremains with my hands, though Mariah reached right in and threw a handful onto the water, which I couldn't help but feel was a slight against my fussy inability to hold our mother's body and bone dust. Mariah wanted to be more real than me, more willing to get her hands dirty, this time literally. The ashes gummed up at the edges of the water, rolling in with the tide, coating the grass. By the end, after several scoops each, we ended up dumping the rest of the box directly into the water. I didn't feel at peace by the end, exactly, but at least we'd left her somewhere private. No child would come up from a dive covered in her mud and particles of bone. Her ashes would sink to the bottom of the ocean and remain alone and undisturbed, just how she wanted to be and never was.

During Mariah's last visit to Bobbie's, before she started to remove herself from my life for good, I don't remember her ever even looking out the window at Willow and Stefan's house. I don't remember her ever going over there or expressing anything at all about it, at least not to me. I thought this was strange at the time, but we didn't have that easy freedom to speak our mind that we did before what happened that summer, so I said nothing. We had parted ways with a hug and promises to call each other, but soon after, she had changed her number or abandoned her cell completely, and then, one day a man answered, telling me I had the wrong number, that he didn't know anyone named Mariah.

She called me a little over a year after Mom died, at my workplace in the history department. I worked as an assistant to a youngish new professor whose work was on 1920s witchcraft in the Ozarks. During his office hours, young women waited outside, hoping he would notice them, hoping to please him. I felt bad for them. They seemed foolish, and desperate, so I would often let them wait in the office with me instead of outside in one of the many chairs that lined the space between his door and the next professor's office.

Luckily, Mariah had caught me during a rare dry spell, no students in sight and only me in the office.

"I'm about to get on a plane," Mariah said. "I just wanted to say goodbye before I go."

"To where?"

"Back to Zurich. I'm doing that Jungian dreamwork degree I told you about, remember?"

"I remember," I told her. "I just didn't know you'd even gone or come back. I haven't heard from you in a year. I wish we'd had more time to talk before you left."

"You've gotta stop worrying about me," she said, her voice tight "I'm not a child anymore, and even when I was, your worry never helped me or yourself."

"I'm sorry," I told her, unsure where her anger was coming from beyond the usual old wound. As I was speaking, I knew it was the wrong thing to do to bring it up here, with thousands of miles between us, but I couldn't help but say it.

"If you're talking about that summer, you have to know I was trying to protect you."

She made an unidentifiable sound and the line crackled, the receiver too close to her mouth.

"I know that's what you think you were doing," she said, "but you were really only jealous and lonely. I know so much of what motivates you is out of your awareness. I forgive you, but I also know you aren't present enough to be in my life right now the way I need you to be. That's why I'm going to do this program. I want to know every part of myself. You want to be ignorant to parts of yourself. That's okay, that's the way it is right now, but I can't be like that anymore. I have to make everything that happened mean something. I can't let all those ruined lives be for nothing."

That was how she felt about me, that everything I did or said came from some dark, tangled source that she couldn't be near, as though I were filled with poison. She had gone from being angry with me for a choice I made to feeling sorry for me.

"They were wrong," I said, simply. "They were sick people. I'm not perfect, and you're right, I'm not as brave as you, but at least I gave a shit about you enough to stop them."

As soon as the words came out, I wanted them back. I had a wild thought that because the call was at such a distance, maybe they hadn't reached her yet, so perhaps I could get them back, pull them up through the perforations in the receiver by the black roots and ball them up and throw them in the trash, but of course, I couldn't, and her sharp intake of breath told me she'd heard them and they'd hit her just as I'd hoped in that hot moment: she was hurt.

I don't think I'd as much as said Willow and Stefan's names out loud to her since it happened. I'd never blamed them or her, not since that night, when everything went wrong and I had to spend hours in the police station, explaining what I'd seen and what I knew, after Mariah had been dragged through the whole process, too, and we were sent back to our lives, now in different houses, going in completely different directions.

"I'm sorry," I said into the silence.

"I know you are," she said.

I felt helpless against her refusal to hear me.

"It's not ever going to be the same again, is it?"

"No," she said. "You took something from me."

The professor chose that moment to walk in on my phone call. I looked down at my hands and saw that I'd scattered pages on his desk, blackened them with tears mixed with my mascara.

I ignored him, even as he came closer and sat down in one of the chairs reserved for student visitors, watching me.

"Do you remember how it used to be? I just wanted it to be like that again."

"Chelsea, you remember everything wrong. Mom was always drunk and you were always gone. If I hadn't found them, I probably would have never known what an adventurous life looked like. Goodbye, Chelsea."

She hung up.

The professor, seated in a chair usually reserved for students, shook his head. "Relationship problems?" He asked, smiling at me slyly.

I remember looking at him and feeling this cold, sharp hatred. I wanted to punch him in the face. I wanted to throw him from a building. Instead of any of those things, I let him take me to his apartment in town, and not for the first time. He called his wife from the land line by the bedside and told her he was feeling ill and was going to try to sleep it off in his apartment and be home the next day. I could hear a baby crying in the background and the frantic sound of her voice when she asked if he was running a fever. He reassured her that he was fine, that he just needed some rest, and then hung up and turned back to me, handing me a glass of whiskey.

"You're lucky," he said. "You don't always have to tell somebody where you are and what you're up to. It's exhausting."

He admired my freedom. It was one of the reasons why he was attracted to me. That, and my ability to be a blank slate, to stroke his ego and ask questions and give away nothing of myself. I could be a fount of curiosity and admiration and youth, even if I wasn't the prettiest or smartest or most charming woman in the room. I'd learned how men with power worked and what they wanted, and what they wanted was somebody to pour their ideas into so they could look back at you and see themselves.

I stared up at the slowly turning fan and decided that I would never come back to this apartment.

I quit my job a few weeks later, after a quick job search and a dozen applications to entry level positions that sounded peaceful and isolated. I ended up working for the local branch of the public library, where I kept records in the town archives section. I liked being up there, laminating newspaper articles and categorizing the yearly dump of ephemera that came in every time somebody important in town died. My favorite task was going through the boxes and boxes of articles written by the wife of a former mayor who had died at the ripe age of 105. She'd spent her life raising six children and writing article after article about how to be a industrious and happy housewife for Christian magazines. Her life seemed buzzing and busy with usefulness, each baby's fat leg or new tooth a testament to her success. I didn't believe in God, but I could believe in hard work as a form of worship. Children seemed a good way to measure your usefulness. Maybe if you raised your children well and kept your house running you could die feeling as if you hadn't wasted your time. I didn't want a house or a baby or even a partner, but I did want something to make me feel useful. So I threw myself into my library work, and later got my master's degree in library science.

I love working in libraries, no matter how disorganized or underfunded or besieged by busybody mom groups and insane state laws. I loved the little enclosed study rooms where teenagers would go to study or make out or both, or traveling business people, using the rooms for Zoom calls, gesturing and shouting into sleek headsets. I love the magazine section with the cloudy, plastic covers we put over the new magazines, and the much-neglected literature sections, where some of the books hadn't been taken off the shelves for years. I liked to pull the particularly dusty ones out to page through them. It felt wrong for books to go unread for so long. The library felt safe, a place that could contain everything and hold every contradiction, unlike real life, where I so often felt forced to pick a side.

July, 1999

Wake up, Mariah said.

I opened my eyes and I was still on the couch, the sun shining down on me through the curtain that I'd pushed aside that morning, hoping the hazy sunlight would invigorate me. Now, I was too warm, my neck twisted painfully to one side, face flushed.

Mariah came into view, leaning over me and brushing aside my sticky hair. No shadows through the window. I'd slept for hours.

"You ready to wake up yet?" She asked me.

"Why aren't you at work?"

"Lunch break," she said. "And I wanted to check on you. I've never heard of anyone taking a nine AM nap. I figured you must've needed it." I sat up and Mariah hugged me close to her. She smelled like musky perfume and sunlight.

"I put on Willow's perfume," she said, noticing me sniffing at her hair. "She lets me get things from her room sometimes and try them out, her robes and such. Just like Cassandra used to. Do you like it?"

"It smells...old."

"It smells ancient. Like a bottle of perfume you'd pull from a tomb."

I nodded, though something about the way she said it made it clear she'd heard this phrase from somewhere else. "It suits you," I said. "You seem kind of ancient yourself."

Mariah wrinkled her nose and shook her head, feigning offense. "You think I look *old*?"

"Old in a good way," I said. "Like sleeping beauty, only in that bed for a hundred years, her hair growing all long and tangled like yours, never aging." I reached out and snagged a length of her hair, as tangled as I'd imagined it would be, and we both laughed. I'd been pulling knots from her hair since she was a toddler.

"They want you to come over again for dinner later this week," she said, hugging me tight as she said it, maybe anticipating how little I'd want to go in my current mood. "They insisted I bring you. They really like you."

The idea of anyone liking me seemed ridiculous in that moment, but I hugged her back, feeling the warmth from her body flood through me.

"Sure," I said. "I don't think I'm going to be up for dressing up this time."

She smiled. "They like you no matter how you look."

I took the next day off of work and then the day after I had off anyway, so I had two days to bum around the house and feel sorry for myself. I didn't want to set foot back in work after what had happened with Jackson. I had the urge to just call and quit on the spot and try my luck somewhere else. I tried to resist it, though. I wish I could say I resisted out of a desire to be loyal, to stick with a job I'd committed myself to, or to challenge myself to deal with a difficult situation, but truthfully all I wanted was to show Jackson that my feelings weren't hurt, that I was supremely unbothered, that I was still cool with everything. I wanted so badly to be cool and not embarrassed. But I needed a few days to get back on track.

Each of those days, I rode my bike to the nearest beach, a rocky shore where you could jump from a jutting rock and into the water from about twenty feet up. I hadn't done it myself and didn't plan to, I couldn't trust that there wasn't a piece of metal or rock or branch or broken shards of a boat jutting up, waiting to impale me or tangle me up and keep me under the water, no matter how many other people I saw jump into the water before me. I watched a pack of teenage boys run from a distance and jump from that height into the water, some tucking their knees up to their chests, some diving down in a straight line like Olympic swimmers, others flying from the edge with their arms and legs still pumping wildly. They all landed, some with a slap against the water, others with a tidy splash as their bodies disappeared beneath the surface and then emerged again.

Still, I wouldn't risk it. Somehow, their lack of injury made it feel even more likely that I'd end up with a broken leg or worse — they all made it, so now the statistical likelihood that I'd be the one who got hurt seemed higher. All of that good luck had to run out eventually.

July, 1999

That weekend, Mariah and I went to dinner next door. This time, Willow greeted us. Her dress was flowing, as usual, but now she wore three enormous necklaces, stones at the end bouncing at her chest. She was slightly sweaty, as though she'd been exercising just before I came to the door, but what she'd really been doing was drinking: her cheeks were so red I thought maybe she'd made a mistake with her blush, but then I saw her sloshing large glass of wine, clearly not her first, and understood.

"Oh sweetie," she said, "I've been cooking all day for this. I'm so glad to see you."

She reached out to press me against her and some of her wine spilled onto my collarbone. She reached out and wiped the wine with one finger. She put the finger in her mouth, licking it away.

"Can't let it go to waste," she said.

I nodded, dazed. I felt a little sick to my stomach, but also excited: everyone was in a strange, secret mood, I could feel it as soon as I walked into the room. I looked at Mariah, who beamed like Willow did, only as far as I knew, she hadn't drank at all that afternoon — she'd mostly stayed with me, helping me dress in something comfortable yet presentable, giving me slices of cold cucumber to put over my eyes and lipstick to brighten up my face. But looking back, I felt the same energy bouncing off of her, too — a little unsteady, boundaryless, and manic, a word I'd learn later in life for the feeling of driving fast in a car down a road that first seems wide and limitless but quickly narrows and cramps until you know you'll eventually have to crash on order to stop the momentum.

Mariah drifted away from me and opened the kitchen door — steam rolled through and she disappeared inside to tend to some boiling pot. I saw Stefan in there, briefly, as the door swung shut. He reached out his arms to embrace Mariah, though I didn't see him complete the motion because Willow pulled me away to the art room, where she placed me in front of a painting-in-progress.

"Look," she said. "Do you see who it is?"

I didn't at first. The kaleidoscopic swirl of color at first obscured the image, confusing my eyesight in ways that weren't exactly pleasurable.

This painting was different from her usual mixed media or fantasy art for book covers. It was maximalist, filled with vibrant, painful color. I looked at the painting for a few seconds before I identified the image, edged in blues and reds. I saw the outline of a woman, her hair streaming behind her, her eyes the only recognizable thing, at first, then the planes of her face assembled.

"It's Mariah," I said, but I didn't say it with wonder or delight, but fear. This was a Mariah on fire, fearful and enormously proportioned, lording over the other, barely discernible objects in the picture: a window behind her, streaming violet sun, and a bowl of the fruit on the table, the contents illuminated as though irradiated.

Willow didn't notice my tone. "I was inspired the day we came home after a date," she said. "Mariah dozing here in the living room, the moonlight through the window. I had to paint her immediately."

I nodded. "I wondered why she didn't come home on time that night."

Mariah had lied to me about what had happened that night. Seeing this picture, I couldn't understand why. She'd allowed them to paint her. What had kept her from simply telling the truth?

"Your sister is a marvel," she said. "So good with the kids, but she's done something else for us, too. We've come alive since she started working here. We both feel so inspired and animated. You've done a wonderful job raising her."

I turned to her, surprised by my own offense at my mother being erased.

"I didn't raise her."

Willow nodded, eager to soothe me. "Yes, I didn't mean it as a slight to your mother. I mean, when she talks about home and who she admires, all she talks about is you."

I nodded, but the night continued to feel off-kilter. Willow drew me near her. I smelled her strange, earthy perfume and the wine on her breath. Her skin was warm everywhere, and when her shirt gaped open, I saw the curve of her bare breast. I looked away, embarrassed, feeling a flush of shame about something, but I couldn't identify exactly what I'd done to warrant it.

II

January, 2017

I stepped aside to allow the agents to enter. I kept the baby on my shoulder as they questioned me: she was a form of protection. I held onto the irrational belief that nothing terrible could be said or done while I had the baby in my arms, an old superstitious holdover from my childhood, when I would make up complicated rules that would keep everyone alive and well — if I woke up before everyone else, they would be safe. If I walked the same path home every day from school, we would all be okay. Every day, the news itself proved me wrong, as women and children could still die wrapped up in each other's arms, but I can hold both the truth and my illusions at the same time.

"We have a few questions about Mariah's whereabouts," Wheeler said. He nodded toward the couch. "Can we have a seat?"

I nodded, wishing I'd brushed off the dog hair and bothered to clean up the magazines and books. I could do nothing with the baby on my shoulder, but Collier smiled at my obvious embarrassment and swept away the magazines and books herself.

"I remember when I had a little one," she said. "I had people nearby to help me. Do you have anyone?"

I shook my head. "My mother died years ago. My aunt lives in Massachusetts. She visits when she can but she's getting older and doesn't travel much. My dad, I never knew him. I looked him up a couple of years ago and found he had died in a car accident when I was still a kid. And my sister, as you know, isn't around. My husband's at work right now — he helps a lot, when he's here. But during the day, it's just me."

Jesus, I told myself, *shut up*.

Collier nodded, adding, perfunctorily, "It must be hard."

"It is," I shrugged, "but babies are hard for everyone, family around or not."

"So Mariah never comes to help?"

I had to remember, all she wanted to know about was Mariah. I should give nothing else.

"No, I haven't seen her since well before I had the baby, before I was even pregnant. She's called since then, but never came here."

"We spoke to your aunt Bobbie. She told us you both lived with her for a while before you set out on your own. Makes me think she might be close to Mariah."

"Yeah, we stayed with her, but it wasn't for long that it was both of us. I lived with Bobbie when I was in college and she lived with our mother until she graduated from high school."

"Do you think Mariah has been in contact with your aunt Bobbie?"

I shrugged. "If she has, she didn't tell me." I was confused by the question. "I thought you said you'd talked to Bobbie already?"

They both nodded. "We just wondered if maybe she'd told you about a phone call or visit that she might have forgotten about."

"No, I don't remember anything like that." They were trying to trip me up, see if either of us was lying. I felt my heartbeat surge, but breathed deep to keep the panic from rising. If I let it get bad, if I let my body start to reveal my fear, then I'd draw their suspicion even more. I couldn't help it: the police made me feel guilty even when I knew I'd done nothing wrong. I held Faun tight and breathed in the clean scent of her.

Collier nodded. "Okay. We'd like to ask you a few more questions about your sister — anything would help."

"I don't understand," I interrupted, holding up a hand. "I haven't seen her in over a year. It's been months since she even talked to me on the phone. Last I heard she was living somewhere in upstate New York, but we don't...we don't talk all that much anymore. I'd like to know where she is now just as much as you would."

The baby stirred on my shoulder. She'd want to eat soon, and as much as I supported women breastfeeding wherever and whenever, I felt vulnerable pulling my breast out in front of these detectives.

Wheeler spoke again. "We know she's part of The Friendship Circle. They're under investigation for illegal activities in several states. We have reason to believe your sister might be involved with these activities."

I knew about The Friendship Circle already, but I'd had

no intention of telling them that. "Do you mean she's done something illegal?"

Wheeler shook his head. "We don't know anything certain yet. We can't say more than this, unfortunately. What we need you to know, though, is that we've come to you for any information or insight you might have in order to help her. We are curious where your sister might be right now, but we'd also like to know more about her to create a profile to better understand what her part might be in all this, and how to help her out of this situation."

"What kind of situation do you think she's in?"

Their oblique questioning, how blank their handsome faces stayed, made me uneasy. I imagined I could stumble into admitting something I didn't intend to, the way they just sat there, impassive. I didn't even know what I might need to hide from them, I knew so little of Mariah's life now, but I reflexively wanted to protect her. And, as far as I knew, federal investigators weren't truly in the business of helping people in trouble as much as finding people who had broken federal laws. Jesus. What had she done?

They exchanged a glance that told me nothing and then turned back to me. The woman spoke this time.

"I know this must be a shock," she said. "Your sister isn't in any trouble, not right now, but we have reason to believe that she might be involved in something much bigger than she understands, something that might be putting her in danger. We'd like to help her out of that danger."

I should have heard this for what it was, an obvious attempt to engage my empathy, to make me want to give them information that I might otherwise be too canny to give. Surely, a part of me understood this. Another part of me looked at the kind face of the FBI agent, her brown eyes lighting up when the baby cried, and wanted somebody to help bring Mariah back to me. Maybe something as serious as the threat of arrest could snap her out of it and bring her home.

I'd watched a few documentaries about cults in the years since Mariah had started living with The Friendship Circle. Mariah herself had once pointed out that I have the opposite of whatever drew people to cults. I am naturally suspicious of people joining up in groups — it makes me nervous to watch church services or sporting events, everyone chanting the same words, joy and anger and righteousness flowing. Feels like the more people you get together, the more potential there is for that emotion to run hot, to turn bad, to twist reality into something heightened and strange. Put a leader at the head of it and that risk feels even higher. So perhaps I over judge what is cultish and what is just normal human community. I was willing to entertain this idea, that I'm just particularly averse to collective joy. Too much joy feels risky.

Still, after Mariah told me about The Friendship Circle, I found myself researching utopian groups, new religious movements, and cults. As much as I wanted to trust her, her certainty spooked me. I watched a documentary about a yogi who gradually began to exert control over a huge number of otherwise intelligent people, a group full of Master's degree students and spiritual seekers in the late 70s. They had ecstatic experiences, ones they still, even years later, believed were in some way real. *I experienced God*, one of the former members said, her face taking on a faraway look, a slight smile raising the corners of her mouth. Suddenly, she was no longer in the room discussing the ways she'd been abused (the mind control, the sexual abuse, how she had to crawl into her guru's room on her knees because she was a woman). Despite all of the abuse, there was some kernel of joy. Not just a kernel, but an explosion. That explosion of joy was, of course, what made the abuse possible. I watched another about a group that took over a Western town, and another about David Koresh, who filled a bunker in Texas with multiple wives and eventually multiple children. Most of them died, from a fire started by the overenthusiastic ATF officers or from being fed poison by their parents. I listened to the Jonestown massacre audio while feeding the baby and making dinner. I heard the children crying in the background, a woman screaming to leave and the rest of the group telling her no, assuring her that there was nothing left for her if she didn't complete the ceremony, that life as they knew it outside of the commune was over.

    I was shaky for days thinking about how easy it is to make a person feel that they are alone in the world, that all they have is this one group, sometimes even just one person with the key to happiness or heaven or connection, that's the one that really seems to get people, a feeling that they are truly and really connecting to something larger and better than themselves. Families can do this: I felt it myself when I was a very small child, and then I had lost it. How happy most people were in the little cocoon of family, and how outside of that happiness I felt since then. Maybe my essential loneliness was a gift. I was not the kind of person who would be vulnerable to a cult because it was impossible to believe I could ever fit with a group of people. Until Colin and I started dating, I imagined I'd be alone most of my life.

Still, maybe it was only by a whim that I hadn't turned to something bigger than myself to subsume me, as it seemed Mariah had. I resisted these thoughts, though: it was hard to think uncharitably about Mariah, to imagine that I had somehow arrived at a better place than her. It seemed objectively true, since no federal agent was showing up on her doorstep to identify my whereabouts. Still, I couldn't see my Mariah being the kind of person who could, for example, hold down a child and force poison into their mouth. I couldn't see her believing the words of a guru or crawling on her knees to bring him tea, the cup balanced perfectly on her back. I could see her, though, becoming addicted to the feeling of connection with another person, connected to some universal understanding that came like a lightning bolt. In all the documentaries, the former members of a cult long for those moments of joy, even as they realize what had been taken from them and rage at the person who took it. Mariah wanted to feel whole. If The Friendship Circle made her feel whole, then I could see her doing something terrible to keep it in her life.

"My sister is one of the most gentle people I've ever known," I told the detectives. "Whatever she's doing with the Friendship Circle, she's doing because she believes she's doing something good. I don't think she's capable of violence."

"People who think they are doing something good are the

people most capable of violence," Wheeler said. Collier gave him a look that said *cool it*, and took over the questioning.

"That's the kind of thing we want to understand, Chelsea. We need insight into her character."

I shrugged. "I'm not sure where to begin with that."

"Then tell what you've learned about The Friendship Circle first," Wheeler said.

I told them what I'd heard from my research. The Friendship Circle is a leaderless movement. It has its own form of scriptures, created by an anonymous group of core individuals about twenty-five years ago. The scriptures themselves struck me as harmless, the usual new-agey stuff about oneness, mystical visions, lots of claims about community as the highest form of worship. The Friendship Circle, as its name might indicate, is about the need for fellowship. They believe that being solitary and cutting yourself off from the community is a kind of sin that depletes your soul, that eventually destroys you. They trace every major evil, from school shootings to genocide to loneliness, and explain every instance of groups gone wrong (Jonestown being the best example) as groups poisoned by the desire of a leader, not blessed with that third, godlike spirit that comes naturally when a group is together in one place in an honest, loving way without ego.

I understood that it wasn't the writing or dogma or even life instruction that called to people as much as the act of being in one of the communities. The Friendship Circle held daily dinners at their shared homes, open to anyone invited. The invitations were never completely open, but people who had the same "frequency" as other members (judged by the members themselves — their scriptures put an enormous emphasis on intuition and trusting it beyond anything else).

"Have you heard much of anything about the, shall we say darker, side of the group?" Agent Wheeler asked.

The group had a few detractors, among them a former child star who had first credited the group with getting her off of drugs and on her feet, then later described them as controlling and sadistic, requiring her to get up at four in the morning and kneel on a fine layer of rice for hours until her knees were bleeding. This was after a heroin relapse, she told a smooth-faced television reporter when she finally re-emerged from her self-imposed silence. She had a delicate, heart-shaped mouth that I couldn't help but watch as she spoke and enormous brown eyes. She still looked like her child self, which I remembered well from my own childhood, but all of her girlish characteristics had ripened into adulthood, her huge lips and eyes making her look like a human doll. The actress wept in front of the sympathetic woman, who then pivoted to questions about the woman's current sobriety and showed clips of her stumbling down the street a few nights before. The woman wept again, in shame as the newscaster watched her with expert objectivity, waiting for a break in her crying before asking another question about her sex life.

Beyond her, the complaints were few, and since The Friendship Circle had no centralized authority and complete independence based on the shared home a person happened to be at, it was hard to pin anything on the organization itself. Sadistic leaders existed, but so far, they had been driven out by their groups before anything serious happened. The group never tried to defend those who were called out for abuses because there was no reason — no hierarchy needed protecting, so if somebody was a source of trouble, they could easily be removed.

"I haven't heard much," I told them. "Just that one child actor who was on TV last year. It seems pretty idyllic, to be honest. A thing you enter into freely and then leave when you want to."

The detectives nodded, their faces showing nothing.

I realized, all of a sudden, how exhausted I was, and that I could not keep my thoughts straight. My shoulders and jaw had tightened. I opened my mouth and shrugged, feeling the telltale pain run down my back: I'd been bracing myself for something terrible. But they had nothing to tell me. They were looking to me for answers, and I didn't have them.

"Is there any way you could come back tomorrow, if you have more you want to know?" I asked. "The baby is due for her nap and I'm exhausted."

They exchange a glance. Collier clicked her pen shut, then nodded to Wheeler.

"Sure," Wheeler said. "And if your sister happens to call between now and then, please keep our visit to yourself. You can understand why we might want to be discreet."

"I still don't understand what kind of trouble you think she's in," I said.

Collier took over again. "I can't give you specifics, for reasons you must understand. Your sister's name came up."

I nodded. "Okay," I said. "I'll tell you if she calls. But I doubt she will. She hasn't called me in so long."

Wheeler nodded. "I understand that. What's most important from you is insight into who she is and what might be motivating her. Once we understand that, we can better know how to help her leave and keep her safe."

They kept talking about safety, an idea I don't truly believe in. But it was comforting, nonetheless. It wasn't until they left that I started to shake from the fear and anxiety I'd held back for the last hour. I went upstairs with the baby and got into bed and beneath the covers until the shaking stopped.

July, 1999

I remember feeling uncomfortably hot and already tipsy by the time we sat down to eat, over an hour after we'd arrived at Stefan and Willow's. First, I only had a few small sips of a full wineglass they'd left in front of me, but before I'd realized it, I'd drunk the whole thing. Willow and Stefan and Mariah were all giddy, too, leaning into each other like old friends at a bar. I watched them as if from a distance, marveling at such intimacy. Willow reached over her food and touched Mariah's hair. A sleeve from her dress dragged across her plate and soiled the hem. She didn't notice. I could see them trying to include me, making gestures in my direction, verbal and otherwise, but I saw them through some fog. The heavy, ugly feeling had crept back in, and being in a room with so many people who seemed to care about each other made me feel even lonelier than I had the last few days. I wasn't filled with a moral shame about what had happened with Jackson. I was annoyed at myself for even bothering with him and tainting my summer so early with disappointment. It was more a complete failure of my desire to be somebody new. I felt like the same old fuckup, misreading everything but not knowing how to fix it. I looked down at my food and tried to manufacture an appetite.

"Tell us about your mystery man," I heard the words drift across the table. Stefan was asking, though Mariah shook her head at him, trying to redirect. Willow caught on and tried to stop him.

"Stefan, don't bother her about—"

"I'm just curious," he said. "I'm a fan of young people getting as much experience in love as possible."

"He's nobody," I said, and liked the sound of that. "We don't share any kind of love. He's just practice for real life."

This stopped the room. I remembered then that the children were at the table, too, so I couldn't say much else.

"I've never heard a person described like that before," Stefan said. He looked at me with interest, like I was a new species or baffling piece of art. "When will your real life begin?" He asked. "I wonder if we're real or just practice, too."

My cheeks burned and I felt admonished. This was probably the wrong way to think about people.

"What I mean is that it's nothing serious. Just a friend."

"Chelsea's never had a real boyfriend." Mariah seemed to be racing to my defense, but the words burned. "I don't know why she hasn't. She's so beautiful and smart and my favorite person in the world. She's real…choosey." I didn't want to talk about any of this, especially around the kids. I glanced over at them and saw that they'd stopped listening to us. They fed the dog under the table and talked among themselves about a book all three of them were reading together, something about children who traveled

97

between dimensions to visit each version of themselves and save themselves from various disasters.

"I'm not interested in a relationship right now," I said, hoping this would shut down the conversation.

Willow nodded, winking at me. "Let's leave Chelsea's love life alone tonight," she said. "We're making it seem like a person needs to be in romantic love to be happy. There's all kinds of love, and all kinds of ways to be happy. Relationships can be... complicated, can't they?"

This question was directed at me.

"I guess they can," I said. "I just haven't found somebody I want to know all that well. And maybe nobody has ever wanted to know me."

I regretted my honesty because all three of them looked at me with what looked like pity.

"Oh honey," Willow said, putting her arm around me and pulling me close to her. "If somebody doesn't want to know you, then that's their loss. You surprise me with new depths every time you come over. I wish you'd come more often."

Stefan moved toward me as well, placing his hand on my shoulder.

I wanted to resist the touch, to shut it down and get myself out of the hug and throw off Stefan's hand, but another part of me couldn't pull away. I was tired of my own inability to want just one thing at one time.

Stefan was to my right, his mouth near my ear. I felt his long hair brush against my throat. "Mariah has become such a part of our family," he said. "I wish it could be like that with you, too."

I let Willow press me against her and nodded. "I'd like that," I said.

Mariah and I waited in the living room while they brought the kids upstairs. It was adult time now, and the kids knew to not come down until morning. We curled up on their increasingly food-stained couch and wrapped up in the musty, dog-smelling blankets.

"They're such cool people," Mariah said. She was braiding my hair, tugging gently and smoothing it. I felt sleepy. "I hate the way you've been the last few days, crying over some asshole."

Some asshole. "How did they know about Jackson?" I asked. I was drunk, which was having the alarming effect of making me feel sensitive, stupid, and wronged instead of happy or numb.

Mariah shrugged. "I told them you were feeling down and they wanted to know why. I didn't tell them everything, just that you'd been seeing a guy and it didn't work out."

The warmth I'd felt momentarily when I'd let myself melt into Willow's arms had worn away, leaving a vague embarrassment. I didn't like the idea of these people, basically strangers, thinking they knew me as well as Mariah knew me, or of them having ideas about my life or what I should do with it. Also, if they knew it had gone badly, why had they asked? It seemed almost cruel, or at least designed to create some kind of reaction in me. If they'd wanted me to feel better, why bring it up at all?

"I wish you hadn't told," I murmured, as Stefan and Willow

bounded back into the room, flushed and excited.

"We want you to come see our new paintings," Stefan said. This was directed at me, though Mariah jumped up, nodding, dropping her half-finished braid. "This is truly our first collaborative painting," Stefan said. "And Mariah's part of it, too."

Stefan stepped forward and held out his hand for me to hold. He hauled me up onto my feet and pulled me near him, knocking over a glass of wine in the process.

I looked down at it, distressed, but Stefan waved his hand at the growing red stain.

"It'll be fine. The painting's the thing now."

I couldn't think of anything I wanted less than a new surprise, but Stefan held my hand so tightly, pulled me next to him and forward, so I followed anyway, too drunk and demoralized to resist. The alcohol had hit me in that way it sometimes does, where I suddenly feel cut off from everyone else, behind a fog. I tried to beat the feeling down. Mariah was only trying to invite me into her new circle, and Stefan and Willow wanted me there, too. I owed it to myself to try. I told myself this as Stefan led me through hallways, seeming to pull me closer and closer until we were touching, my shoulder to his chest, him with his arms nearly wrapped around me by the time we reached Willow's art room.

Willow and Mariah were already there, giddy, leaning into each other.

This was a new painting, one that had been hidden earlier. A near-naked woman was seated on a couch, dirty-blonde hair fanned out around her shoulders, her body tilted slightly forward, her head thrown back, eyes looking at the viewer with something like defiance. A piece of fabric lay across her chest and genitals, draped strategically to cover her. It wasn't finished, though — an empty space remained next to her.

Mariah.

Seeing the surprise on my face, Mariah came closer, standing between me and the painting.

"I meant to tell you," she said, flushed. "Willow and Stefan are painting me, and they want you in the painting, too."

"Our muses," Stefan said. "You both inspire us so much, we've been creating every day, just putting on Alice Coltrane records and painting until our hands hurt. And every painting is, in some way, about you girls."

I looked at the painting and felt a curious unease. She was nearly naked. Not naked, not completely, but nearly.

Beyond Mariah and the easel was a couch, same one as in the picture. Two robes were draped across the cushions and two folded, silken sheets, iridescent in the last rays of sunlight.

"I've been wanting to paint you two for so long," Willow said, coming up behind me and grasping my shoulders. "The night we came back from a date and Mariah was here, I had the idea — she was asleep on the couch when we got here, she looked so angelic, so innocent, I just had to ask if I could paint her. I finished that one and almost immediately started this one, too, with a spot left for you."

Mariah had moved away from me and toward the couch. She sat down, listening, and placed her hand on one of the robes for a moment before grabbing it and heading to the bathroom attached to the room.

Willow had stopped talking and looked at me, waiting for a response.

I don't know what my face revealed, but my mouth said "It's beautiful."

It was beautiful.

Something beautiful can't be bad, I thought. I remember that thought because it was the first time I knew I was having a thought meant to keep me from following my instincts.

"I am so glad you like it," Willow said.

"Would you be willing to be part? I've got an empty space there. I'd love for you to fill it."

"It's just," I took a deep breath, feeling myself redden even as I tried to stay cool. To be that adult woman I was trying to be. "I don't know if I'm supposed to let her pose like this. She's fifteen."

Stefan gave me a look I imagined he reserved for philistines, for people who looked at contemporary art and said things like "My kid could paint that" while standing in front of a Rothko.

"Chelsea, she's not naked — we made sure she felt safe, that she was covered up."

Willow crossed her arms and I felt the air change. I'd said something wrong.

At that point, Mariah walked out of the bathroom, the robe loosely around her front, but untied.

"Mariah," I said, turning toward her, trying to pretend that it was just me and her, to ignore what felt like a growing, dark cloud over where Stefan and Willow watched us. "Are you okay with this?"

Mariah shrugged. "Yeah. I think it's cool."

I nodded. She seemed not annoyed exactly, but surprised that I would have any questions.

"We'd be happy to talk to your aunt," Willow said, turning to Stefan. I saw something cross his face, some moment of hesitation, but then he nodded.

"We don't want either of you feeling awkward," he said. "If you think she'd disapprove, of course we'll let her know. And of course, if you don't feel comfortable, Mariah, we don't have to finish. We can end the painting now."

Mariah looked back and forth between me and Stefan.

"I wouldn't feel right continuing the painting at all if Chelsea's not comfortable with it either," he said.

Mariah turned to me, her eyes already wet and pleading.

"Please, Chelsea. I didn't think you'd react like this…it's just a painting."

Mariah turned away from me and made her way to the couch. She didn't ask me what I feared, why I was upset. She didn't seem to care what I thought, only whether I would allow her to do this thing. I was outside the circle. The sun was slanted, nearly in Mariah's eyes. A portion of her face was bright, nearly invisible in that light, while the rest was in darkness. I'd spent enough time with Willow and Stefan to know that the good light was rapidly leaving, that they'd want to seize the moment now if this painting was going to happen at all. I was quite literally wasting their time.

Mariah patted the place beside her. "Imagine what it will be like to look back at this painting when we're older," she said.

"We're never gonna have an opportunity like this again."

These sounded like somebody else's words, but maybe they were true.

Willow went to the window, where she lifted a length of fabric up and behind a hook, letting the last bit of sun in.

"I promise it's not so scary as it seems," Mariah said. "They're gonna make you feel comfortable. And this is what you are wanting, right? You're eighteen. You're leaving home. You told me you want to be different. This is different, a painting we'll look at for the rest of our lives and remember who we were then. I want to do something special together."

"I'm not leaving," I protested. "I mean, not really."

She shook her head. "It's not the same when you don't live at home," she said. "It's gonna be different. And it's okay, but I want something to remember this summer."

When Willow and Stefan came back, entering the room mid-conversation, mid-laugh, I wondered why I had been so afraid. They had offered to talk to Bobbie, after all, though Mariah and I had both ignored the suggestion. Talking to Bobbie might reveal other things, like how often we drank wine, and that I'd not even realized Mariah was being painted in the first place. Still, if what was happening here was so awful, then would they offer to talk to Bobbie about it? And here they were, two people who loved each other like I'd never seen any adults love each other, except maybe Cassandra and Bobbie. They were the healthiest, happiest adults I knew, and here I was, about to blow an opportunity to do something I'd probably never have an opportunity to do again.

I was lucky, really, I thought as I stepped into the bathroom, undressed quickly and completely, and threw on the robe. Stefan left the room as Willow twisted the cool, slick fabric around us, wrapping us up in it. The sun slanted directly on our backs, warming us, making the back of my neck tingle. He came back in when Willow shouted that she was done. She'd posed us with our heads leaned together, collapsing into each other like two dolls discarded by a child.

Willow blocked out my proportion in the painting while Stefan stood in the background, watching, stepping in every few moments to convene with Willow about some detail or to gently, carefully turn our heads, shoulders, or lay our hands in a better position. After an hour, the sun had nearly disappeared and Stefan turned on all the indoor lights so Willow could complete a few last details.

The harsh, yellow light made the room shine differently. The fabric wrapped around us was iridescent, but milky, the shining threads woven like tinsel through the weave of a cheap Christmas sweater. The smell of acetone and ammonia came from the work desk in the corner, where the paint thinner and water cups were jumbled together, hardening brushes twisted on the counter, the whole area dark and littered with unidentifiable objects and globs of hardened paint. I looked down at my feet, which were dirty, the bottoms dusty. My back hurt, my neck hurt, and when I looked down, I could see the shadow of my breasts beneath the thin fabric. I wanted to go home.

Stefan noticed my shifting. "I think the girls are done for the day." Willow looked up, saw my squirming, and nodded.

Stefan left again, as Willow unwound us and we got back into our clothes.

We left at ten, longer than any dinner should have lasted, but Bobbie trusted them, and she trusted me, and it was the summer, a time when teenagers were supposed to live a little, do some things that aren't exactly what one is supposed to do, wasn't it? We walked out, past the paintings and family photos, past the kitchen, where plates from dinner were still on the table. We walked out the front door and into the dark, cool lawn, the grass damp, the air moist, and the night loud with bugs, a deep, mechanical throbbing coursing through the air until we got back home and shut the doors against the busy, thrumming night.

February, 2017

Mariah called me two weeks after the agents first came. She was uncharacteristically to-the-point.

"Has anybody contacted you?" She asked as soon as I answered the phone.

I paused only for a beat before answering.

"What do you mean?"

"I mean, has anybody asked about me? Bobbie, even, asking where I am."

I almost told her. It was tempting to have some truth to tell her, to let her know I was loyal to her and wouldn't keep secrets. But I remembered the words of the agents, that they were trying to keep her safe. I didn't trust them, but I trusted the idea that they might give her preferential treatment if she arrived with evidence, with a finger to point at somebody else.

"No," I said. "I mean, Bobbie asks about you because you never call her, but nothing unusual. Is something wrong? Would there be a reason people are trying to find you?"

Mariah sighed. "Whenever you are trying to live in a new way, when you expand your mind beyond all of these arbitrary social norms, people try to destroy you. You of all people know how that goes."

"Why don't you come and visit?" I asked, ignoring the last part. "Faun's getting so old now. She's getting a tooth, even."

Mariah's voice softened. "I wish I could," she said, and I heard the truth in it. "But I've got too much to do here,"

"With The Friendship Circle?" I asked.

"Yes," she said. "But by the way you say I can tell you think it's ridiculous, or a cult, or just misguided, like everyone else."

"I don't know what it is," I said. "You've never really told me what it means to you."

"It's just a lot of people who want to make their lives better. Who want to live as a community. It's not run by one person and nobody is in control of anyone else. And that's why people hate it — we refuse to live like everyone else, we refuse to be part of some bullshit hierarchical structure. The 3-D world is a lie. The only sane thing to do is leave it."

This was the most she'd ever told me about the group, even if it sounded like the official "about us" section of their website and not genuine thought. She'd never even tried to recruit me, and remembering this brought forth that old pain of separation.

I imagined she didn't want to recruit me because she didn't want me so close or didn't think I was the right kind of person for it. And it was true, I wasn't the right kind of person. I couldn't imagine sharing a house with a group of people I didn't know or even ones I did know. Even eating in front of people made me feel uneasy. Colin was the only person I could do any of those things around, and even that had taken months. Still, the idea that she hadn't asked me reminded me of my own shortcomings. I would like to be the kind of person who could throw down a sleeping bag and make myself at home anywhere. In truth, I'm the kind of person who gets upset when I meet an acquaintance in the grocery store and have to make small talk.

"If it's so great, why haven't you encouraged me to join?" I asked, knowing this was the wrong thing to ask.

She paused. "I...I didn't think you'd be interested."

"People in The Friendship Circle stand in airports and on streetcorners trying to get people to join them, yet you are really picky about inviting me."

This was such a terrible, pointless road to go down, the guilt road. But I felt like my mouth had been hijacked by somebody trying to say the absolute worst things. I remember once I'd taken a class about early American literature and they'd talked about the idea of an imp, an idea that came from Poe, that we all have this imp inside of us who is destructive, who turns us away from the things that would do us the most good and guides us toward our own destruction. I tried to shoo the imp away but he was clinging to my shoulder, whispering in my ear.

"You can find a chapter in your area," she said, her voice soft, almost sad. "It's local — you don't invite people from other places. If you're interested, you can look up the closest group."

My imp liked having her on the defensive like this, having to respond to my questions, feeling trapped, but her timidity scared me. I had wanted her to get angry, at least. To begin a conflict that could escalate so much that we'd both feel something intense at the same time. This is what you call *negative attention* when a child does it. How useless it is to know a thing but feel helpless to stop yourself from doing it.

"Apparently you're just down the road. If you think this is the best way to live, then come and tell me about it yourself."

"Upstate New York is a pretty big place," she said.

"Not so big that you couldn't come visit."

"I want to, Chelsea. I really do. And when I can, I will."

"Please come soon," I said. My voice was wobbly, and what had started as a way to draw her out became real, raw need. "I don't want you here because I'm lonely. It's been that way in the past, I know. I want you here because I'm happy, finally happy, and I want you to share in it. I miss you."

Mariah spoke softly. "I'll come when I can, and soon," she said. "I'll try to arrange it, okay?"

"Okay,"

"I love you," she said. "No matter what happens, I love you."

I said the words back, but the shock of it only hit me after she hung up. She hadn't said she loved me since the summer of 1999.

Collier and Wheeler showed up a few days after Mariah's call. I thought about what to tell them about the call, if anything. When they asked, I told the truth, but only part of it.

"She asked if anyone had come asking about her. I told her no."

Wheeler nodded. "Good choice," he said. "If we've got

any chance of getting her out, then she can't know we're looking for her."

I was surprised when they immediately started to ask me about the past, about the summer when we lived with Bobbie, instead of the call.

I stopped them before answering anything. "I don't understand why we're talking about this."

"We need to know who Mariah is, that's the only way to get somebody out of one of these situations," Collier said. "To know something personal, to know what makes her tick."

"Like, you want her deprogrammed?" I asked.

Collier shifted uncomfortably and looked at Wheeler.

"Something like that," he said. "We don't use that word anymore, it's got some bad connotations. It's more about reminding the person of who they were before the cult, what connections they've lost and what the cult has taken from them."

I shook my head. "Before The Friendship Circle, Mariah had me and Bobbie and nobody else. And she didn't trust me, not since we were teenagers. She was alone. That's probably why she got interested in the first place."

"Tell us more about that last summer that you two lived together with your aunt," Collier said, leaning close to me. "What you started telling us last time. You can go get the baby if you need to." Faun had started crying, wailing from the bedroom.

I nodded and went to the bedroom, where she was on her hands and knees in the crib, crying, raging, but also crawling, which she usually refused to do.

I took her in my arms and soothed her until the only

111

remnant of her crying that remained was little sniffles and hiccups and her wet, clumpy eyelashes. I took her with me, softly snoring, as I went to tell the detectives about the summer when everything fell apart.

July, 1999

When we got home that night, Bobbie had already gone to sleep, the book she'd been reading left on the table, open and bent at the spine. I had half-hoped she would be awake. A part of me wanted to tell her what we'd been up to, to see if it truly was as okay as it had felt in those moments before they turned the indoor lights on. It had felt enchanted, adult, the kind of feeling you read about in a book and think *that's life*. That's real life, a special thing happening and feeling completely, and fully alive.

And then, at the end, it suddenly turned poisonous, awkward, ugly, despite nothing really changing. How could I trust such a fickle instrument as my feelings?

The problem had to be me.

Still, in the days after the painting, I started to feel a stickiness in my mind. The memories got stuck in my head like a song. They'd come back to me all at once, that moment when the sun was down and the room lit with bulbs instead of sunset, when everything started to feel tawdry, to feel wrong. Without fully knowing I intended to, I kept my distance. When Willow asked me to come over to pose again, I made excuses, excuses that

I could tell she saw through, but I didn't know how to explain my feeling, didn't trust my own feeling to be worth explaining to begin with.

Back at work, I did my best to ignore Jackson, though he sometimes invited me to smoke after work anyway. He caught on, eventually.

"Listen," he said, "I'm sorry about what happened the other night. I promise I just mean talk, nothing else. We can hang and smoke like we used to. Everyone else here is so boring."

Everybody else in the restaurant included a couple of ambitious high schoolers saving up money for college, a few people like me and Jackson, in-betweeners who were waiting for the next step or supporting a non-paying ambition (I remember a musician and a painter, both of indeterminate age), and a smattering of older folks who either enjoyed the late hours of working at a restaurant or simply couldn't find a better job. I suspected a few of them had drug problems that involved things much heavier than weed, though they never talked about it, and on the days they stumbled late into the backroom, bleary-eyed and nauseated, the boss would let them throw up quietly out behind the dumpsters and had us cover their work until they were able to be back on the floor or kitchen again.

When I think back on it now, there was something beautiful about the complete acceptance we had of each other, the old addicts and high school students and drifting, aimless people like me and Jackson. But at the time, the thing with Jackson ruined my good feelings about work. All I could feel was this filmy, sticky sensation, as though I'd walked through a spiderweb. I wish I'd had the courage to just leave. I didn't know that leaving could take courage. I thought courage meant staying with something no matter how terrible it made you feel and how much you wanted to crawl out of your own skin while doing it.

"I don't really come to work to talk," I said. "I'm just here to do my job and leave."

Jackson followed me out to the dumpster, where I threw out one of the many bursting bags from the night. It had been a busy weekend, all blue skies and eighty-five degrees for three days straight, sticky, lingering heat that even our proximity to the ocean couldn't cut. I felt sick from the heat and the smell of garbage and wanted nothing more than to go home and sink into the claw-footed bathtub.

"I'm sorry if what happened wasn't what you wanted," he said. "I didn't mean for it to end up like that. I don't want to ruin our friendship."

Jackson, king of terrible timing. Any other day, I might have been glad to hear his apology or at least his acknowledgement of how I was feeling. That day just the sound of his voice made me want to pick him up and throw him in the dumpster along with the stinking bag of scraps.

"Friendship," I repeated. "Friendship would mean you asked me about my life sometimes. I know plenty about you, down to where your girlfriend works, but you don't know a thing about me because you never asked. And you never asked because you don't give a shit. And that's okay — you don't have to. But please don't pretend you do. I'm not here to help you with your boredom. I've got my own life and it has nothing to do with you."

He looked down at the ground as I spoke. This infuriated me even more. He looked bashful and sensitive, as though I'd hurt his feelings and he couldn't stand to look at me. I almost laughed: I had hurt his feelings by telling him the truth. The only lie I'd told was that I had my own life.

Mariah noticed my distance. In the week or two after the painting, after I turned down multiple invitations to come over in the evening, Mariah came up to my room one night, after dinner, and asked me what was wrong. I was reading a book at the time, the diaries of Anaïs Nin. Nin had reconnected with her father after years of estrangement and they'd made vows to be devoted to each other. He asked her to let him be the only man in her life. It made me think about our father, a man I vaguely remembered, who Mom claimed probably had a whole new family or was long dead, a John Doe in a gutter. I know her anger came from feelings about him and whatever had happened with him (she never gave details except that she'd chased him away with a rake in her hand and thrown his clothes in the dumpster). I had a probably apocryphal memory of him in that dumpster, the metallic bang of him kicking against the sides in anger.

"Chelsea," Mariah said my name, breaking the spell, and tugged at my exposed foot. I was in my bed, under the blankets, reading from a flashlight. I didn't have to read like that, I just enjoyed it. It made me feel like a kid again, in my own, warm nest.

I disentangled myself from the blankets and poked my

head out. There was Mariah, her cheeks sunburned from being outdoors with the kids all day, her hair down and wild.

"What's up?"

Mariah shrugged, a sure sign that whatever was coming next was hard for her, made her preemptively want to brush it aside. "I notice you haven't come over to finish the painting. You've barely come over at all."

I sighed and dog-eared my book, setting it down on my overflowing bedside table. She was playing with the ring she wore, one I had given her for her thirteenth birthday, the day she became a teenager and joined the club. It was a cheap, glass version of her birthstone, a garnet. It was fake, but still held the deep, blood-red hue of a real gem.

She looked up at me. Her eyes were enormous, and red. She'd been crying. Suddenly, she was crying now.

I pulled her to me, surprised. "I'm sorry Mariah, I didn't know you were upset."

"Do you think they did something wrong? Is it bad that we did that painting?"

I paused, unsure what to say. Who was I to say what was wrong? I was the only one who felt some intrinsic wrongness, and I was no expert on right and wrong, as I'd so quickly proven.

"I think what matters is how you feel," I said, finally, thinking this would be the only way for Mariah to understand, if I could just get her to feel the sticky, heavy emotion that I did. "Do you feel like it's wrong?"

Mariah was still in my arms, and I could almost feel her thinking — could feel the flurry of thought in her head, the pressure, the tension throughout her body. I waited for her to say yes. I badly wanted her to say yes and to immediately stop working over there. I wanted us to move on with our summer, without this family having such an outsized role in it. I wanted my Mariah back.

"No," she said, simply, just when I thought she wasn't going to answer at all. "I didn't feel bad until I thought maybe you did."

I nodded, brushing her hair away from her sticky, tear-stained face.

"Well," I said, "then I think that means it's wrong for me, but not for you."

"So you don't mind how much time I spend with them?"

I shook my head.

"No," I said. "They feed you, they take care of you, they love you like family, right?"

Mariah nodded.

"So that means it's okay. As long as you feel good over there, it's okay."

I have berated myself for years for these words, these silly, weasel words that attempted to have it all ways. I wish I hadn't elevated what felt good when we were raised by a woman who killed herself in the pursuit of feeling good or at least momentarily less miserable.

Not long after that conversation, Mariah started spending most weekends over at Stefan and Willow's. Some nights they left, but most nights, they didn't. It was as though she had been waiting for my tacit approval, my little nudge across the line for her to become truly attached to them.

Bobbie noticed her frequent absence. "Do you think it's okay she's spending so much time over there?" She asked. "Why do they need a babysitter if they're home half the time?"

"They work funny hours. She's watching the kids while they work, even if they're still home."

Later, when I told Colin about this summer, back when we started dating, he asked me why I had kept every worry to myself. Why hadn't I told the one stable adult in my life about my fears, even if I wasn't sure if they were founded?

"You knew something was wrong. Why didn't you tell her?"

There he sat, confused by my baffling inability to say what I feel, to reach out to the adults around me for support. It made me feel very tender toward him, and jealous, too. Here is a man that learned early that people would listen to him, that he was safe. As much as that left something openhearted about him, it also left him unable to understand what a luxury safety is.

"I've kept secrets my whole life," I told him, working it out as I spoke. "We had to hide our mom's drinking so that nobody would take us away. We had to take care of ourselves. Keeping secrets was my default and it had served me well. I didn't want to take anything away from Mariah, anything good. We had so few good things."

So it's not surprising that I hid a lie behind a truth when Bobbie asked me what was going on.

She was looking at me, still searching my face for signs of lies, for signs something was wrong. She was a practiced hider, too. As was my mother. Maybe she could tell I was keeping something from her, but she wasn't sure what.

"I think they really like her and want her to be part of their family," I told Bobbie, shrugging. "They're just really warm people who can see we are a little...lonely. Plus, of all the people Mariah could be spending time with, two artist college professors doesn't seem like a bad choice."

For Mariah, at least, there was an expiration date: she moved back in with Mom at the beginning of September, when school started up again, and that was just a few weeks away. What was the harm of letting this whole thing play out and allow her a few more weeks of happiness? Perhaps this is where Bobbie's mind went at the time, to how little joy or stability we had.

Bobbie let it go, again. She'd thrown herself into the garden and the house since our conversation about Cassandra, so she, too, was in her own world of pain and reckoning. She'd weeded the garden, pulling away long roots and chunks of soil, clearing way for tomatoes and perennials that had previously been choked by the bittersweet and pepperweed and chervil. She had bought a perimeter of wrought-iron fencing and installed it with an enormous rubber mallet all by herself on a day when both Mariah and I had been working. She'd cleaned out her closet as well as the liquor cabinet (she hadn't commented on the missing alcohol) and all of the kitchen drawers, where she had shown us ancient treasures, like Mariah's sippy cup featuring Ariel and a cup covered in moons and starts, which had been my favorite until I was too old to admit to a favorite cup and it was lost in the collection of abandoned things that gathers in every old house.

    She'd been busy that summer putting herself back together. It was no wonder she allowed me to take on the responsibility of taking care of Mariah.

February 2017

After I finished telling Collier and Wheeler the thumbnail of what happened with Stefan and Willow that day, I put Faun down for a nap and came back out to find them readying to leave. I didn't tell the ending, not yet. I wasn't ready to speak of it, and they didn't push me, either. They had files and files of testimony to look at: they surely knew how it all ended. Maybe they didn't need me to talk about the crime, but everything that happened before it.

"Wait. You've got to help me understand what kind of danger she's in," I said. "This isn't exactly my favorite topic of conversation. It would help to know why I'm having to revisit this."

Dragging up the events of that summer was beginning to eat away at me, create a permanent, acidic pit in my stomach. The last time I drove down the mountain to town for groceries, I'd felt on edge, and thought I saw someone who looked just like Stefan, like Willow, even like Mariah, around every aisle. I walked up to a pile of gleaming cucumbers, their waxy skin dotted with moisture from the produce spray, and for a moment was convinced that

Mariah was standing there, her back to me, bagging up a spiky artichoke. She was blonde, slight, and humming a song beneath her breath. When she turned, I saw it wasn't Mariah — the woman was ten years too young and freckled, but my heart didn't stop beating until I got home and forced myself to nap with Faun.

I thought I detected a small nod from Wheeler to Collier.

"You're right," she said. "We should be more open with you. Truthfully, there's not much concrete to say. We suspect some leaders of The Friendship Circle in three bombings of private citizens. We were only able to connect the group through one of the leaders of the upstate New York chapter. The leader in the area calls himself Agape. We saw Agape in surveillance video from the post office. He mailed one of the bombs personally, the first one. His appearance matched that of the man we'd seen in videos circulated by former members of the Friendship Circle. We suspect your sister is involved in this inner circle."

"Is there only one group around here?" I asked. I echoed Mariah's earlier words. "Upstate New York is a big place. How can you know she's involved in that particular group?"

"It's the only one," Collier said. "There are a couple of groups in the city, often living in abandoned or condemned buildings, but upstate seems to have only one major hub, reportedly located in an abandoned house in the mountains, off the grid and off our radar. If she's here, she probably knows something about what's going on and why certain people are being targeted by Agape. That's what we can't figure out, why he chooses these targets and how he convinces the rest of them to go along with it. If we knew that, then we could stop him."

"You think she's part of it. These bombings."

Wheeler shook his head. "We don't know the extent of your sister's involvement, but we know she is a better ally to us than enemy and that she could get uniquely close to Agape. We hope to offer her a deal."

I didn't like where this was going.

"You mean she's in the kind of trouble she has to deal her way out of."

Wheeler held out his hands, making a gesture of helplessness. "We just don't know. That's why we need to talk to her."

"Who were the targets?" I asked.

"Private citizens," Collier said. "People who you'd think would have no connection to a cult leader."

I nodded, noticing that they had only strategically answered my question. They didn't want to tell me too much.

August, 1999

One night, in early August, Mariah spent a rare dinner and evening with us. By August, she spent most evenings as well as days with Stefan and Willow, though she'd always come back to sleep in her own bed. Bobbie had gone over to talk to Stefan and Willow and had apparently been satisfied enough to say they seemed nice, and the children were very happy, so she didn't see a reason not to let Mariah enjoy the summer. She didn't like Stefan, though. "Seems full of himself," she said, a devastating thing to be in Bobbie's eyes, but she liked Willow. Said she was warm. She suspected Mariah needed that warmth, that motherly love.

That night, when Mariah walked through the door, Bobbie exclaimed "Our May Queen has returned!" and raised her water glass as though to make a toast.

Mariah wore a dress covered in flowers and her hair hung loose and long. She did look like some kind of harbinger of Spring, though at this point it was late summer, and I could already feel the season change ramping up, the fruits all too ripe, the trees too green.

Mariah laughed and asked for a plate.

We ate together and Mariah filled us in on the details of her week. She'd helped with the children's homework and done loads and loads of white laundry, which was now hanging on the backyard line, moving back and forth with the wind as we spoke.

"I love doing the laundry," she said. "It's relaxing. My brain just drifts away."

"You could do it here, too, if you're looking for some real zen," Bobbie said.

Mariah told us about all of her plans for a little patch of garden next door, how Willow had brought her to a local organic garden center that had all the best plants.

"You can tell they are in a good place because everything is healthy and blooming. Stefan said the plants can tell if they are cared for by people who love them."

I couldn't help myself: I rolled my eyes. "Weird how the plant I never water in my window keeps growing when I don't give a shit about it," I said.

Mariah glanced at me, then back down at her food.

Bobbie had stopped paying attention to us and walked over to the sink to scrape her plate clean.

"I'll see you girls in the morning," she said. "I'm gonna crawl into bed with a book. Mariah, I expect some of those magical plants around the house soon. There's some space for planting over here, too, after I wrestled away all the weeds"

As soon as Bobbie left, Mariah turned to me. "You don't have to be mean," she said.

"I'm sorry," I said. "I just get sick of hearing about them. Bobbie did all the gardening, did you know that? Even after we promised to help?"

Mariah looked up at me, her mouth twisting. "Actually, I did know that. I'm just next door, remember? I see Bobbie everyday. It's you who's gone, even when you're here."

I looked back down at my half-eaten plate, no longer hungry. Maybe I was distracted, maybe I was gone. But at least I hadn't left her for a whole other family.

"I just miss you."

"I know," she said, putting her hand on mine. "I'm not really gone, you know? I'm still here. You've just gotta come meet me in the middle. You never come over anymore. They miss you. Willow even asked if they'd done something wrong or made you feel bad."

"What did you say?"

She shrugged, looking away from me. "I didn't know what to say. I didn't want to hurt their feelings."

I nodded. I didn't want to hurt their feelings, either.
"I'll go talk to Willow soon. I just needed some time. I promise I'll make it better."

I had a night off, and I didn't know what to do with it. I was keeping my distance from Jackson, so I had little else left but reading alone in my room or watching television far into the night. Sometimes I'd go into town and wander around the bustling main street, hanging around outside of bars and asking for cigarettes. I couldn't go into any of them because I wasn't of age, and unlike in movies, people really did care about that, no matter how adult I thought I looked in my black eyeliner (which I now recognize, as inexpertly applied as it was, probably made me look younger than my age, and ridiculous). That night, though, I didn't have the heart for it.

Mariah pushed aside the covers to get in next to me. Her skin was cool and she smelled of the outdoors. It was the dress, it smelled like the air because it had been dried on the line. Mom had insisted on line drying everything in the summer, up until just a few years ago, when she saved up money for a dryer. Line-drying had been one of the last holdovers from the person she'd been before.

"I was thinking about something today," Mariah whispered. "Remember when Mom brought us out for ice cream and she got into a fight with that guy at the stand? It was summer, and she was wearing sunglasses inside the place because her eyes were all bloodshot, but she took us out anyway."

"Is that when she threw her ice cream at the guy? The guy who..."

"He commented on my legs. I was ten, and he said something about how with legs like that, I'd better start wearing longer shorts."

"Oh god, yeah. What an asshole." I remembered the man, balding, wearing a baseball cap. I thought I remembered him being with a woman roughly the same age, probably his wife, but she stood silent next to him, intervening only after Mom threw her sundae at him and got us banned from that particular Friendly's location.

Bitch she hissed at Mom as we left, and I remember wondering why that woman didn't defend us, why her husband deserved to be there more than we did.

"Mom never let people make us feel bad about stuff like that. She let us wear whatever we wanted."

"Yeah, that was one good thing about her."

We were speaking as though she was gone, when really, she was just a half hour drive away and I'd called her the day before but hung up after fifteen minutes made it clear she was beyond having a conversation. At six PM I should have known better.

"I'm sorry about how I was acting down there," I told Mariah. "I don't know why I did that. I guess I still feel weird about what happened and I don't know what to do with that feeling."

"I get it." Mariah reached out and put her hand over mine. "It *was* weird and I should have given you some warning."

I wondered what kind of warning she could have possibly given me.

"Can we just watch a movie together or something?" I asked. I wanted it to feel like the old days for a little while. She nodded, and we curled up in my bed and watched the VHS of *Little Women* that Bobbie had picked up for us, the one where Claire Danes plays Beth and cries so beautifully when she tells her sister that she's not afraid to die, she's just sad that everybody else is going to grow up and leave her behind. We fell asleep together and I woke up alone: Mariah had gone to work and slipped out without waking me.

March, 2017

Telling Wheeler and Collier about that summer had sent me into a strange, abstracted mood for the rest of the week. I grew distractible, forgetting to eat all day and then being surprised by a wave of gnawing, angry hunger at night, or neglecting simple things, like tea kettles that I didn't discover until the water had almost burned away and coffee cups left all day in the microwave.

When I was studying history in undergrad, I became obsessed with the idea of history not as a series of events, but a construct that changes depending on who tells the story, what part of the story is highlighted, and when the story is told. That's beyond the first layer of history, the one we accept most willingly: history as a static thing that represents some inevitable patterns of events that lead us here, where we were always meant to be. It felt revelatory to me to realize everything is framed, everything is made into a story, and knowing this made me feel like I'd escaped from Plato's cave. I studied the philosophy of history, even considered getting a Master's degree, hoping to continue my obsession with the way history is told. I didn't end up applying to the program. I realized I didn't have much to say beyond the initial revelation. I didn't want to dive into the idea, I just wanted to see it happening and stand outside of it, to point to the story whenever anyone else got too comfortable with one version as truth. It was another way to be outside of things, to feel I was always above the story. Maybe that's why I became a librarian instead.

I can see that I am telling Mariah's story from a particular perspective, one that is not the truth, but one truth. I cannot really stand outside of it, and even as I attempt to stand outside of it, to create it, I'm creating a new story.

Colin held Faun in his arms. She was crying and we couldn't figure out why. It seemed too early for her to be teething, but maybe it wasn't — I had read a great deal about how to keep a baby alive, how to make sure the baby's nervous system was well regulated, that she saw her emotions reflected in my eyes so she could recognize them as her own, but I had forgotten to read about teeth. I googled *when does a baby first get teeth?* and the answers came up. Six months. Seven months. Twelve months.

"Jesus Christ," Colin said. "Did you find anything out?"

"It could be teeth," I told him. "Maybe she's just getting teeth early."

He shook his head. "Maybe teeth. That fucking helps," he muttered as we walked away, jiggling the baby in his arms.

"Touch her gums, see if they are hot or swollen."

"I'll try, if she'll ever let me."

Colin was in a mood. So far, I've painted him as angelic, almost saintly, but that's not fair to the real Colin, who is neither of those things, at least not all the time. He's as difficult as me in many ways, so cheerfully devoted to the idea that everyone can understand the world if they just have enough information, enough communication, that he refuses to see the brick walls, the blocks, and tries to blithely walk right through them. He doesn't believe in a place beyond the ability to communicate, and unfortunately, that's often where I live. He's also very kind and forgiving, both of himself and me, particularly since we had a baby and can often be thin-skinned, exhausted, and likely to snap at each other.

I held my arms out. "Give her to me and take a walk outdoors for a minute. I can tell the crying's getting to you." He nodded and handed her to me. He didn't even bother to put on a coat, just walked out into the cold with the dog.

Faun was moaning now, occasionally making a sharp screech of pain. I put my finger in her mouth and moved it around, feeling along her gumline. She quieted down as I explored, gently pressing down against my finger, then harder. I found it, then — a bump beneath the skin, a hard bit of bone trying to emerge. I pressed, and to my surprise, she calmed.

"That's it, isn't it?" I asked her, watching her big, brown eyes clear of tears for the first time in an hour. "Just a tooth tearing its way up through." She gummed my finger hard, the pressure relieving the pain.

I wished we had a bottle of whiskey to rub on her gums, but Colin doesn't drink and I was breastfeeding and didn't drink hard liquor anyway, so I kept my finger in her mouth and rocked her until her eyes closed and her grip on my finger relaxed. She was asleep. I put her down in the crib, pulling her blankets up over her body. The rest of our house was a wreck, filled with piled up newspapers and overflowing trash cans, but her blankets were immaculate, sweet and powdery smelling.

As I watched her sleep, I heard my phone sound from the next room. An unknown number. I assumed it was spam, but answered anyway. Mariah had called from an unknown number last time.

I thought I heard distant voices, but wasn't sure. I was listening so hard for some background sounds, some indication of where she was, that it took me a moment to notice how long she'd been silent.

"Are you okay?" I asked. I knew it was her.

"I want to come see you," she said. I couldn't get a read on her feelings. Her voice wasn't flat, exactly, but it was subdued, as though she were trying to betray as little emotion as possible. It made me wonder who was listening to the call.

"Okay," I said. "I want to see you, too. When can you be here?"

"I can't say, exactly. I've got some things to take care of before I head out. But soon, within a week or so?"

"You can't give me a day?"

"I'm sorry, I can't. Don't worry about cleaning the house or anything, I really don't care about any of that. I just want to see you and Faun."

She paused and we both waited, feeling something grow between us.

I thought about the agents, waiting for my word. I didn't intend to tell them anything. As soon as Mariah told me she was coming home, I knew I would protect her. I didn't care what she'd done.

"I am so happy you're coming," I said. It was true, and the truth of it made me tear up. "I want you to meet Faun so badly. And Colin."

"I've missed you, too," She said. "I didn't mean — I didn't mean everything I said before. I've been so mad for so long. I don't want to be like that anymore. I'm ready to release it all."

"Maybe you can come live with us," I said, rushing, as always, pushing her too far too quickly. "Come help me with the baby. We could raise her together — Colin could be our babysitter so we could go out to one of the bars in town on the weekends and play sad country music on the jukebox and you could get the home phone numbers from all the loggers and mechanics and college professors in a twenty mile radius. It's just like the commune, only we have electricity."

Mariah laughed. "Sounds like a dream," she said.

"It does," I said. I could really imagine her here, rocking the baby at night, waking in the morning to drink coffee and read the paper with me, wearing a silky robe, her hair long and spilling on the table. I had a sensible haircut, a chin-length bob that I got right before Faun was born, foreseeing that I wouldn't have the time to do much with my hair from now on, but I'd live vicariously through her indulgence. She'd bring some glamor back to the house, and maybe some of it would rub off on me, too. I pushed the thought of the agents, of the cult, of the criminal activities she was part of. We'd deal with all of that somehow. I would hide her in the basement if I had to. I'd buy her a tiny home in the middle of the forest behind us and carve out a path that only I knew.

I heard a flurry of voices in the background, one shouting her name.

"I have to go," she said. "But I'm going to see you soon, okay? Within a matter of days. Week at the most."

"Love you," I answered.

"You too," she said, and hung up gently.

August, 1999

I was home alone when I got the call from Mom. I had a day off, mid-week. While Bobbie was off having lunch in town with her library group, I was in my pajamas eating cereal from a plastic tupperware bowl that had been stained red from old spaghetti sauce. I was watching a talk show in the background, something about teenagers with black lipstick, black hair, spiky collars around their throats and shoes with thick, black soles getting makeovers so they looked more like regular teenagers. One girl, her lips lined dramatically in black, looked younger with her face scrubbed, dressed in flared khakis and a button-up blouse. She stared at the camera, smiling, but about to cry.

"I look pretty," she said. "I've never felt pretty with my regular face before."

The audience clapped as the young woman wrestled with the realization that the mask she'd worn had hidden somebody she didn't recognize, and that this self was somebody even the flaky, sometimes violent audience could love. The host hugged her, either genuinely moved by her tears or recognizing an opportunity to look more human herself. She pushed up her enormous, red glasses and told the camera they'd be right back with the next transformation.

Then, the phone rang. It was nearly noon, so I was surprised to hear Mom on the other end, her raspy voice communicating that not only was she already tipsy, she might also have a cold.

"Hey Mom," I said, already uneasy. "What's up?"

"Something need to be up for me to call my girls?" She asked, her voice already with an edge of defensiveness. How dare I imply she shouldn't call. How dare I imply she should only call if something was wrong.

"I'm glad you called," I said, sidestepping the question."We've missed you."

"Have you now?" She asked.

"Yeah."

"Hmm. Funny, if you're so excited to see me, then why am I getting letter after letter in the mail about you going to college near Bobbie's, at the community college over there? What's so good over there? Here in town you could go to the four year."

I hadn't remembered that the letters, the pamphlets, all of it would come to Mom's house, and hadn't considered that she'd open them. When I was home, I got the mail from the box and sorted junk from bills. I guess now that I was gone, she was doing the job for herself.

"I don't think I can afford a four-year college," I told her. "I can't get a good enough scholarship to cover it all. And I'd never ask you to pay for it."

She made a dismissive, snorting sound on the other end.

"You coulda done anything you wanted," she said, her

voice fully angry now. She was furious. It had been hard to read her tone through the phone, but now I realized I'd made a terrible mistake even beginning the conversation. Mom was drunk, at noon, and had convinced herself of something, and there was no arguing her out of it. "You want to hurt me. That's all."

"I'm sorry I didn't tell you my plans. I figured it's a good time for me to move out and start my own life. It's hard to do that in the town where I grew up."

"Why? You've got something to hide?"

"No," I said, the old helplessness setting in. There was nothing I could do at this point except try to get off the phone as gracefully as possible. Best case scenario was that she'd wake up in the morning and forget anything had happened. Worst, she'd drink all night and then wake tomorrow even more convinced of whatever she was convinced of now.

"So you'd rather live in that ratty old place with an old dyke, that's better than living with your mother?"

I flinched. "Don't talk about Bobbie like that."

"Oh, I forgot, *Saint Fucking Bobbie*. She can call me a drunk, but I dare say anything about your angel, your saving grace, then I'm the bad guy."

"Well, Mom, you are a drunk, so she's not wrong there."

"And she's a dyke."

"I guess everyone's speaking the truth today," I said, on the verge of tears despite trying to stay angry, to get myself to just hang up the phone on her.

If I'd been home, I could have seen her mood coming, could have anticipated it and soothed it.

"How about you just stay at your Aunt's house when it's time for Mariah to come home," she said.

"You don't want me home?"

"You don't want to be here. You want to go to college so bad out there, I bet Bobbie will do you a favor. She was always trying to poison you against me anyway, her and Cassandra, making you girls feel like there was something wrong with our house, with our lives."

"Don't go there," I interrupted. I couldn't hear her talking about Cassandra, not the way she was right now. They had treated my mother with far more grace than she deserved.

"Oh, you don't want me to say anything mean about the dead? About a stuck-up bitch? She's dead, and I'm sorry for it, but she was never a friend to me alive."

This was too much. I knew I shouldn't bite, that she said it to get me to respond, but I did it anyway. "You've got to be fucking kidding me. She saved Mariah from running out into traffic when she was learning to ride a bike. She'd pick me up from school on days when you were too fucked up to make it. She did more for you than you'll ever know because you were too wasted to even remember it. You take and you take and then you expect everyone to kiss your ass anyway."

It had all come out in a mad, ugly rush, and I knew nothing good would come of it. There was a long, silent pause.

"Maybe she did so much for you that I didn't even know about," she said, her voice dangerously calm and cool. "Maybe if you loved her so much you can go fucking join her in the grave."

Then, the line went dead.

I dropped the phone as though it were a wriggling, bloody thing, my stomach convulsing.

She'd told me to die. As much as I knew she was just angry, that she just wanted to hurt my feelings, I couldn't calm myself. I began to shake, shaking so hard I banged my elbow against the counter, hitting my funny bone, which made me shake harder. I crouched down on the floor. I kept my eye on the clock in the kitchen, a clock made of kitchen utensils with a tiny little cocktail fork pointing to the minutes. I counted the second hand going around the clockface five times before I could stand up again.

Bobbie wasn't home, but I couldn't be alone. I walked out the front door, barefoot, to see Mariah next door. I didn't care about running into Willow or Stefan or looking crazy. I needed Mariah.

I knocked on the door and Willow answered, wearing an apron tied over a pair of linen pants and a tank top. Freckles covered her shoulders and arms, as they did her cheeks. She looked youthful, excited, and I hated to be the cause of her face falling, but I was. I stood there with my face swollen from crying, wearing my ratty pajamas, barefoot, still shaking.

"Honey," she said, "come in." She didn't ask what was wrong or what I wanted or needed, she just took me inside and sat me down. She went to the kitchen and brought me back a glass of water with a single slice of lemon drowned under the ice.

"I'm sorry, I'm just looking for Mariah."

"She's out with Stef, they're getting some supplies over in Springfield. They left not more than five minutes ago, so I suspect she won't be back till afternoon."

I had the fleeting thought that somebody should have told me Mariah was gone, that she was only fifteen and shouldn't be just taken from town without some kind of permission, but I was too exhausted to pick up that thought and run with it.

"Do you feel like talking?" Willow asked. I did not, really, *feel* like talking. I needed to talk. I was like a pressured hose. I took a deep breath. I would practice saying as little as possible. None of this was Willow's responsibility. Or her business, for that matter.

"I just had a bad phone call with my mom," I said, shrugging, trying on the motion. "She got really mad at me."

"Why?"

"She's mad I'm going to community college here in town instead of back home."

"Why would she be mad about that?"

I shrugged. It was impossible to explain in a way that made sense.

"She wants me to stay near home. She acts like it's, I dunno, disloyal to leave or something. Like a good daughter wouldn't want to —" I had to stop then, because my body had betrayed me and the shrugs hadn't worked and I was crying again. I hated crying, and here I was, crying more often this summer than I had the whole year before.

Willow pulled me in and held me in her arms. When the last, shuddering gasps escaped my body I tried to pull away, but she kept holding me.

"Hey," she said, "don't feel bad about crying. I'll let you go, but I don't want you to think you have to stop for me, okay?"

She released me and I sat up.

"I'm sorry," I said, rubbing my face and nose dry with the ratty cuffs of the long-sleeved t-shirt I'd worn to bed. It had been cool that night, foggy, but now the fog had burned away and the sun was out. I felt hot, sweaty, and uncomfortable after all that. I was tired of being a spectacle.

"Thanks," I said. "I just needed to get that out"

Willow touched my shoulder and shook me gently.

"That's what I'm here for. You can come to me, you know, when you're feeling down."

I decided then that I'd stay for a minute. I'd push against my usual instincts. What had my usual instincts gotten me? An embarrassing sexual encounter with an asshole from work. A rift with Mariah. The loss of a friendship with the neighbors. If I did the opposite of what came naturally, maybe I could get it right. As if to ease my body into the choice, I lay myself back on the couch, trying to let myself release into it, sink into the softness.

"I know, and I'm sorry for how I've been acting since… since the painting."

"I wondered why you hadn't come over. What bothered you?"

I shrugged. "I don't even know. I just suddenly felt weird. Felt too naked I guess, even though I was covered up."

She nodded. "We were trying hard to make you feel comfortable. I feel awful that you left feeling bad about the whole thing." Willow settled into the couch next to me, tucking her feet under her voluminous pants. She reached out and smoothed a damp hank of hair behind my ear.

"I know you were," I said. "I'm just not used to being so... free with my body."

"I think women are made to feel shy about their bodies. It starts young, that message that we should feel shame about our bodies, shame about how we want to share our bodies with other people."

A little sliver of discomfort came through. I ignored it and nodded. She was right, after all. She wasn't saying anything that wasn't logically true. If I could just hold on to the logic and ignore my stupid, startled body and brain, then I wouldn't be like this. I'd be free, like Mariah, like them.

"Mom said she wanted me to die." I said it flatly, trying to use as little emotion as possible. I'd been holding that key detail back. What's the antidote to shame? Revelation. I'd read this in one of the many magazines Bobbie got sent to her house, *Self* or *Redbook* or *People* or something else trashy.

"What?"

"Well, I was talking about Bobbie's ex, Cassandra, she died of cancer a few years ago. Mom was saying mean things about her, saying she'd never done anything for us. Then, she said if I loved her so much, I could go be with her."

"Oh, honey." Willow touched my knee. "I am so sorry."

"I know she didn't mean it like I'm taking it. I know she'll probably feel bad, maybe she's even trying to call right now to apologize."

"She says a lot of things she doesn't mean?"

"Yeah, when she's drinking. And she'd been drinking."

Willow looked at the clock on the mantel across from us,

and then back at me. It wasn't even one pm yet.

"I know," I said, tilting my head toward the clock. "She's an alcoholic. She can't stop. She's going to kill herself soon."

I'd never said this out loud before. She was getting worse, had been for a long time, but this summer was new. Her disconnection from us, her anger at me for even the idea of leaving, this was a level of desperation she'd not allowed us to see before. I'd barely had more than a five-minute conversation with her since we left, and I'd interpreted it as her not caring, not wanting to know what was going on with us, but now I could see it wasn't that at all. She hadn't been capable of a conversation.

I could feel something building between us. She was going to offer some kind of help. I didn't want any of it. I was tired of being vulnerable in front of this woman I barely knew. A woman wearing linen pants, for god's sake. A woman whose outfit probably cost more than my entire wardrobe, her calculated dishevelment a kind of invisible proof of money. I'd applied new red nail polish and the edges had already chipped away, but her nails were shaped and glossy and colorless. I caught her looking at my shoes: cheap sandals I'd gotten from K-Mart, the plastic platform base cracked, my toes exposed.

"I'm okay," I said, standing up. "I need to go back home, and so does Mariah. Mom doesn't do well without us. We help her stay on track."

"Doesn't sound much like she was on track before you got here."

I shook my head. "I can't talk about this right now."

Willow nodded. "I'm sorry." She placed her hand on my

head and smoothed down my hair.

I left, but allowed Willow to hug me one more time. "Come over any time, okay?"

I nodded, though I didn't intend to come over and talk about Mom or anything else serious with her again. I had gotten what I needed — I'd practiced letting go and had truly done it. I'd shared something with Willow and it had felt good to let her hold me. But what I'd gotten most was clarity. Willow wasn't like us. She saw me as pathetic, my mother a hopeless drunk, Mariah and I were charity cases, not real people. Mom needed me. Mariah needed me. I'd be going back home in a couple of weeks and it didn't make sense to get closer to Willow and Stefan when I intended to devote myself to family. I was going to help her get better. I was going to encourage her to go to rehab. I'd put off community college for a year or two until she was back on her feet and Mariah was closer to graduation. I couldn't leave either of them in that house.

What I felt most, though, was an enormous relief: Willow was safe. Whatever fears I'd had about the painting, whatever discomfort I felt with Stefan, I knew that Willow thought of us as poor kids she had to help, and that she wouldn't let anything bad happen to Mariah.

August, 1999

As it got closer to time to go home, I became quiet. I wanted leaving to be as easy as possible, and gradually stepping away felt like the best way. At work, I was mostly silent: I stopped trying to make friends with the revolving crew of workers over the summer, stopped even exchanging pleasantries with Jackson. I still showed up for dinner at Bobbie's, still did my chores and helped her get the house back to its previous shape (I even devoted an entire day to scraping and repainting the tattered window frames), but I was quiet, withdrawn, focused on my plans. Bobbie had asked me where I was going to stay when I started college, if I was going to go to one of the orientation days, but I was noncommittal. She had invited me directly to stay with her, and I said thank you, but made no promises. I didn't want her to know I didn't plan to attend this year. I knew she'd try to talk me out of it, and I needed to have a plan and a justification before I told her. I needed to be able to show her that I knew what I was doing, that I wasn't throwing away my future to take care of mom, which I knew would be how she interpreted it. I wasn't throwing away anything — I would go to college, someday, but for now, I had to help get Mariah through high school. I couldn't leave her behind, alone.

Bobbie asked me to start having Mariah come home on time instead of spending all day over at Willow and Stefan's.

"It's going to be a big adjustment for her to go back. I think we need to ease her into it by making a more regular schedule over here."

I was their biggest defender, then. I told her that I trusted Willow and Stefan, that Willow had been kind to us. Like a mother, I had said, and truly believed it.

"I think maybe we should let her enjoy time over there for as long as she can."

Bobbie didn't like it, but she deferred to me. Later, when the police asked about this time, they all asked the same thing — why wasn't your aunt more concerned?

I didn't know how to explain it to them at the time, but I understand better now. Every family is a little machine, and our machine ran on independence, on taking care of yourself and keeping your business to yourself. Bobbie, and to some extent my mother, thought the worst sin was putting your nose in somebody else's business. Bobbie knew that if she overstepped, my mother might never let us visit again. The unspoken rules of our family meant that problems were handled by handing them back to the person they belonged to as soon as they surfaced. Mariah was mine in Bobbie's eyes, maybe even in my mother's. I had loved her since she was born. She said I had claimed she was my baby and had tried to pretend to breastfeed her, had once thrown a spectacular tantrum because my mother had not let me hold her, despite being too small to carry that little weight.

We got the phone call from the hospital in August, a week before we were scheduled to go back home. By then, I was tired of the summer. I had a hard time getting to work and had been warned, twice, that I'd lose my job if I was late again. I'd gathered a pile of money in a jewelry box in my room, which I was saving to help us get through the year. It never occurred to me to send any to my mother because I knew exactly what she'd do with it. The call confirmed my suspicions about what she'd been up to while we were gone: she was in the hospital for complications related to her drinking while having Hepatitis C, which I didn't even know she'd had until the call.

"She's stabilized," the nurse told me, "and she wanted me to tell you girls that you don't have to come, but she'll be here for at least a couple more days, if not more, for monitoring. Your mother has not been taking good care of herself in your absence." I heard a hint of judgment there.

"Can I speak with your aunt?"

I called Bobbie to the phone and walked away as she took the receiver, her voice confident and steady as she wrote down the details.

I paced the living room, looking through the windows and across the yard to where I could see into Stefan and Willow's living room, the windows black in the sunlight. I debated whether I should go get Mariah just to bring her bad news or let her continue with her day. It was less the news that I wanted to share than my own fear. Mom had always been the kind of low-level sick most alcoholics are — too nauseated to eat most mornings, constantly in bed with aches and pains, migraines, frequent colds. But this time was different.

I milled around in the kitchen and living room, waiting for Bobbie to get off of the phone, but she kept talking, her voice in its professional cadence, the tone she used when she wanted to show she wasn't going to put up with any bullshit.

I needed something to do with all of my nervous energy. I needed Mariah.

I could almost see the heat of the day from inside, how the greens were too green, everything screaming of summer and fullness, like in this poem I had to read in high school about heaven as a problem, as full of things always right at their peak and never after — *does ripe fruit never fall? Or do the boughs/ Hang always heavy in the perfect sky.* I had to memorize that part and talk about it to the whole class, so I remember it, still. I understood those lines in a new way that day. I was sick of the summer, all the too-sweet wine and sweat and the smell of Willow's perfume everywhere now, a musky, flower-heavy scent that made my nose itch, as though I'd developed an allergy from smelling it so often. I wanted a cold wind to blow through. I wanted a snowy day where all you smell is the snow and the air, clean and bracing.

I decided to get Mariah and force her to at least come back with me to make sure Mom was okay. I couldn't imagine simply leaving her there, hooked up to machines, without the things that sustained her — unfiltered cigarettes and television shows about disasters and diet Coke.

Bobbie joined me in the living room and looked out at Willow and Stefan's house.

"What do you want to do?" She asked.

"We have to go see her. She doesn't want us there because she doesn't want a fuss, but I think she needs a fuss right now. Maybe a fuss will save her."

Bobbie nodded. "Her drinking's going to leave you orphans. I can't let her do this to herself, to you."

"Did you tell the hospital how bad it is? I bet she didn't."

"Yes. They can tell because of the toll it's taken on her body, but I don't think they understand that she's gonna need some real help to stop. I don't think almost dying is gonna be enough."

"What's Hepatitis C? Is it something you get from drinking?"

"Not really. It's an STD. Something she picked up from your father, I imagine."

Bobbie never talked about my father, but her voice was bitter and I could tell she was angry.

"Do you want me to go get Mariah?"

"Yes," Bobbie said. "They'll have to do without her for a while." I sensed something in the tight way Bobbie said this, but I didn't stop to investigate it. Bobbie went up the stairs, calling down to me that she'd pack up our toothbrushes and a change of clothes in case we wanted to stay at the hospital.

I made my way across Bobbie's still-raw yard and garden, whole swathes of dirt newly turned recently seeded with clover to make a soft, dark lawn that would never have to be mown. Willow and Stefan's lawn was wild, mown only when they felt like it. The grasses brushed my ankles, tickling my skin.

As I approached the house, I heard the kids in the backyard and swung back there, hoping to find Mariah with them.

River had an enormous art book opened up before him. He was pasting cut-outs from magazines, headlines and images and tiny words, to make a collage. Sage and Persephone sat in the playhouse, a tarp-covered shed that Willow and Stefan had furnished with an old couch, a kitchen set, and a pile of books which had warped and twisted in the heat and humidity. Sage was reading from *The Wizard of Oz* and Persephone listened as she lay down on the ground, holding her doll up and whispering to it.

What a beautiful family, I thought. Then, I never dreamed of having children or domesticity, but looking at these kids made me think maybe I didn't want to ask them where Mariah was. To tell me where she was meant I'd have to go deliver this news and tear her away from this scene. Here it was, the family she had always deserved, and I was coming to take her away from it.

River looked up. "Hey, Chelsea," he said. "Mariah's inside with Mom and Dad doing art time, if that's who you're looking for."

"Art time?"

"Yeah," he said, "we're not supposed to come in until they finish art time. Usually Mariah comes out and lets us know it's over."

"It's kinda an emergency," I said. "I'm gonna go ahead and knock anyway."

River shrugged. The other two hadn't stopped their story. I moved toward the front door feeling heavy, sticky from sweat. The day felt almost Southern, the heat so heavy that it felt like I was breathing steam.

I stood at the door and knocked twice, harder the second time. I shifted on my feet, restless. I waited for as long as I could stand before I turned the knob and stepped inside. I told myself that I had to find her in order to tell her what was going on. I had every right to go inside in an emergency, so I kept walking, though I didn't call her name. The house was hushed and, as always, seemed as though everyone had left mid-activity, a book opened on the coffee table with a cup of coffee half-drunk, the kitchen table littered with breakfast detritus of napkins and half-eaten muffins. One of the dogs, asleep on the carpet, stood up, stretched, and whined when I entered, but the others looked up and then fell back asleep. The house was hot, they didn't like using the air conditioner, and I felt the stickiness from the outdoors intensify in the stale air smelling of dog and spaghetti and burnt coffee, a half-pot still warming in the glass carafe.

"Mariah?" I called softly. Nobody answered.

I didn't want to shout and scare anyone, cause the kind of distraction that might ruin a painting or break somebody's concentration. As I got closer to the studio, I heard voices.

The door wasn't completely shut. I looked through the considerable crack and saw, in the reddish light reflected through a thin curtain, a woman on the floor, her back to me. Then, the person turned and I saw a woman's body, completely naked. I knew that woman. Not a woman, a girl. Mariah. At first, it was only her body, her face obscured by a fall of hair, but I still knew who she was. Then, Stefan entered my view, pressing himself up by his arms, hovering above Mariah's body. Mariah turned her head and I could see her profile, her mouth opened to meet Stefan's mouth.

Willow, I thought. I had to get Willow. I even opened my mouth to call, but before anything came out, I saw Willow enter, topless, and then her kneeling down to kiss both Mariah and Stefan in turn. That's the moment when I turned away. I didn't want to see what was going to happen next.

I turned and ran, the carpet muffling my footsteps. I ignored the dogs, who knew me well enough not to bark but too well not to follow me as I left. I told them to sit, and then gently opened the door and stumbled out into the sunshine, into that sticky heat, which hit me so hard I felt nauseated. I doubled over on the porch and retched, but nothing came out. I felt a panic that they might have heard me leave and might catch me on the porch, so I gathered myself together and ran across the lawn back to the house. As I ran, I could hear one of the kids in the back shouting at me: *did you find Mariah?*

Bobbie was in the middle of packing her own bag when I burst through the door and ran up the stairs to her room. I tried to open my mouth when she turned to me but I was gasping and wheezing and couldn't speak. She put her hand on my shoulder as I bent over double and gasped until I could get out the words.

"What's happened?" She asked. "What's wrong?"

"They . . . she's naked. She's over there and they're doing something to her."

Just like she had with the phone call about Mom, Bobbie became still and focused immediately.

"Shhhh," she hissed to me, "Tell me what you mean. What are they doing to her?"

"I don't know for sure. But she's naked and they're naked. I saw them."

"Okay," Bobbie said, simply, and walked away to the main room. I sat on the floor, my head in my hands. Later, I wondered if she was so calm because a part of her knew and that part jumped forward to do what needed to be done.

I listened to her going heavy down the stairs, and then a greeting. The police. Something I couldn't make out, then she gave Willow and Stefan's names, their address, and said yes, she's with them right now. You need to come now.

She came back into the room and crouched down next to me.

"Are you okay?"

I nodded, focusing on the woodgrain at my feet.

"I don't know if I should have told. Was it wrong to tell? Should we have called the police?"

"You did the right thing," she said. "I'm going to murder both of them."

I shook my head. "It didn't look like . . . it looked like she was okay with it, you know?"

Bobbie pursed her lips. "She's fifteen and she can't be okay with it."

She saw my doubt and sighed, exasperated with me. "You've got to stop worrying about them. They don't matter now."

Bobbie could do this thing where she turned it off. Willow and Stefan had erred, and so they were nothing to her.

"They love her," I said. "They care about the things she says, about what she loves. They aren't, like, abusive."

Bobbie shook her head. "That's not how love looks."

I understood what she was saying, but I couldn't believe it. I waited to be punished, and when the punishment came I knew I'd deserve it.

March 2017

When the detectives came again, I didn't tell them about the second call. I was weary of their attention, all the fake care.

"I still don't understand why you're asking me to tell you about things you already know," I said. "I know you have access to files from the case."

Wheeler shook his head. "Like we said before, we just want to understand your sister..."

"If you know who my sister is, then you know what happened that summer. You know more than I do, probably."

Collier took over, her soothing voice lowered as though she were speaking to a particularly delicate child.

"We know what the reports say. We know what the charges were, and what happened to Stefan and Willow, but we don't know how Mariah felt about it or what happened to her after. Neither one of you testified on the stand, and Mariah refused to testify against them completely. You know what really happened to her, how she understood that summer. That's what matters to us, how it changed her life."

I let out a short, dry bark of a laugh. "I'll tell you exactly how it changed her life. When Stefan and Willow went to prison, her life was ruined."

I was tired of telling this story to them, in a curtailed version, and to myself, and I was tired of the self I had to remember when I told it.

"How are those events related?" Collier asked. Wheeler sat at the kitchen table with a pad of paper. He looked up, scribbled a few words, and looked at Collier, who continued to shift herself toward me, hands slightly out before her as if to catch me before a fall. "I'm trying to understand how her abusers ending up in prison ruined her life."

I rolled my eyes. I could feel myself becoming a teenager again as the desire to push against these authority figures rose up in me. "She was miserable after it happened and was never happy again. That's just the truth. They abused her, and she loved them. She never stopped loving them and would have never used that word."

Wheeler spoke up. "From what the report says, what happened to her was rape. And she wasn't the first: they had videos, pictures, paintings of girls around Mariah's age. They did it for years. They carefully picked the most vulnerable girls, girls who wouldn't tell, who would think it was normal or would be so desperate for family that they'd go along with anything."

I knew about the other girls. At the time, it was a scandal in town, a scandal that the papers and local television wouldn't stop talking about because it happened in our little vacation town, a place both quaint and also the summer home of millionaires and politicians and actors and mid-tier artists like Willow and Stefan, who had some regional fame. I knew that Mariah wasn't the first because I saw interviews with some of them, now women, who tearfully recounted their relationship with the couple, how Stefan had gradually drawn them closer, how Willow had made them feel safe while Stefan pushed boundaries more and more until sex felt inevitable. They didn't mention Mariah's name in any of the reports because she was still a minor, but everyone in town knew Bobbie, knew that we lived next door. They not only painted the other girls, and slept with them, but they secretly recorded them, too, had hours of footage, labeled by name and year. Mariah was among them. Because most of the girls were at least sixteen, and the age of consent was sixteen in our state, they couldn't be charged for every instance (except the videos).

Another victim, who had only been fourteen at the time, took the stand. She was twenty-one by then and discussed, in detail, how they had hired her first as a babysitter for their children, then toddlers. They told her she was mature for her age. She was special. They wanted her closer, wanted her to be family.

"I didn't want them to touch me. I didn't want to do it, but I felt I didn't have a choice anymore. Stefan told me that freedom meant not listening to other people's rules."

My stomach had knotted up watching her on the stand, her in a skirt and blazer, both ill-fitting, her face red with tears. But at least she was out of the illusion. She no longer believed that Stefan and Willow loved her, that she was special to them. Mariah did, though, and she wasn't here to listen to this woman who had once been just as convinced as she was that Stefan and Willow were the only people who understood her.

"I know what happened." I told the detectives. "I'm not defending them, I'm just telling you the truth, which you said you wanted to know. That's how she felt about it and that's probably why she ended up with this group to begin with."

"Tell me what you mean when you say her life was ruined," Collier said, gently.

"She hated us all. She hated me. She hated the people who took Willow and Stefan away from her, and those people included me. It doesn't matter what they did to her or how many other people they did it to or how much we tried to convince her. Once they were gone, she never let me back in her life, not really."

Wheeler stopped writing on his pad. Again, they exchanged a look, which infuriated me.

"Stop doing that," I said. "Stop sharing some secret that I don't know about."

Wheeler sighed. "This helps us a great deal, I want you to know that."

"Why?"

"We're trying to understand your sister's involvement, and this explains — "

"Was she part of the bombing? Did she do it?"

"We don't know the extent of her involvement," Wheeler said.

I turned to Collier. "What makes you think she's involved at all?"

Collier, who has once been the voice of softness, now became something else altogether. Her voice went colder, more remote.

"We've been keeping some things from you, yes. I won't insult your intelligence any longer by pretending that you don't know that. We needed to know the whole story, to put the pieces together, before we told you more."

"Can you tell me more now?"

Wheeler spoke up now. "Video footage shows a woman matching your sister's description placing at least one of the bombs on a doorstep, disguised as a UPS package."

I felt as though he had taken out his gun and shot me. I was sweating, but also deeply cold. She was doomed if they had footage. I couldn't hide her away or make it better if there was an actual video of her placing a bomb on somebody's doorstep.

"She's going to jail," I said.

Wheeler shook his head. "We don't know that right now. All we know is that she's part of something dangerous. She might not have known what she was doing. She might have been coerced in some way. She might be suffering from..." Wheeler trailed off, snapping his fingers as if to jog his memory.

"What's it called?" He asked, turning to Collier, but I answered.

"Stockholm Syndrome," I said. He nodded.

"Do you really think that's possible?" I asked. "Is that even a real thing?"

Wheeler shrugged. "That's not for us to judge. Based on what you're telling us, Mariah is at least deeply loyal to authority figures she trusts. If she feels invited into a close-knit group, it's hard for her to give it up and it's hard for her to see the ways it's hurting her. Does that sound right?"

I nodded. Though it had been easy enough for her to leave me behind.

Collier leaned forward, engaging me with her eye contact. "Did Mariah ever tell you anything about who the leader of her group is?"

I shook my head. "She never even mentioned a leader. I always thought the idea of having a leader was against the whole project."

Collier nodded. "On paper it is. In reality, there is somebody pulling the strings, he just makes people believe they want the strings pulled, that he's simply the mouthpiece for what they're all thinking. But right now, these bombings, they aren't a part of the bigger mission, apparently."

"What do you mean?"

"It seems personal," Wheeler said. "Only three people have been identified as part of the bombings — your sister, and two men."

Collier and Wheeler turned to each other, as they had before, when wishing to tell me something but debating it. Or seeming to debate it.

"Are you going to show me the footage?" I asked, tired of this dance.

Wheeler hesitated before sliding photographs from the folder he'd brought with him, where he'd earlier removed his old-fashioned, yellow notebook. He placed three grainy, black and white photographs before me.

"Do you recognize this person?" He asked, pointing to the first photo. I was blurry, and she was wearing sunglasses, but I recognized her anyway — Mariah, holding a package beneath her arm as she walked down a street.

"That's my sister," I said, without thinking, and then shook my head: I'd identified my sister in a photograph presented by detectives who were probably trying to arrest her. "I think. It looks like her, but I can't be sure."

Collier noticed my distress. "Don't worry," she said. "We knew it was her: this isn't the only evidence. We have her fingerprints on the package."

"How would you have her fingerprints?"

"Your sister signed up as a substitute teacher a few years ago — that's how we had her prints in the first place."

I focused on the second picture, a man far better at disguising himself than Mariah was. He wore glasses, a hat, and nondescript, baggy clothes that hid his shape, though he was obviously slim.

"I don't recognize him,"

The third photograph was of another man, tall and slim. Younger, probably, and wearing only sunglasses.

"Him either."

"Are you sure?" Collier asked, and for the first time, I heard something like desperation in her voice. She wanted me to know who these men were because she didn't know for sure, unlike with Mariah.

I nodded.

"Now that we've told you more about why we need your sister, do you understand the importance of tracking her down? If she can identify these men, we can get her away from whatever kind of influence they have on her, whether it be Stockholm Syndrome or traumatic bonding or her being devoted to whatever twisted cause these men represent, we could be looking at a reduced sentence."

I didn't have a choice. I had to at least appear to help them. "Okay," I said. I breathed in and felt my feet on the floor, the only solid thing in the room. "How can I help?"

"Maybe she'd believe we honestly want to get to the truth if it came from you. Maybe she'd be more willing to come forward."

I shook my head. "I'll do whatever I can to help, but she doesn't trust me. Nothing coming from me is going to persuade her."

"So you wouldn't consent to a televised plea? Seeing you wouldn't motivate her to turn herself in?"

I laughed. "I can't think of a worse idea to be honest. If she saw me on television, asking her to come forward, she'd get as far away as she could. She needs to know she can trust me, and something so public like that is so out of my character she'd immediately know you were behind it.."

"Listen, Chelsea," Collier said, glancing at Wheeler before continuing. "If things are as you say between the two of you, if she is so angry, then we need to consider that you might be a target."

"A target of what?"

"These bombings are of regular citizens. Just regular people. We haven't put together exactly what connects them, but if Mariah has something to do with choosing the victims, and if you are as estranged as you say, you could be in danger."

I shook my head. "That's not possible," I said, and when I said it, I believed it.

August, 1999

I closed my eyes and waited until heard the front door shut. When I knew Bobbie was gone, I opened my eyes and went to the kitchen. I found a note on the counter — *Went over to get Mariah and meet the police. You stay here.*

I went upstairs and lay on the floor next to the bed and stared up at the ceiling, watching the fan's blades blur together, watching a fly bounce around the lightbulb, looking for a way to enter the light. The floor was solid and cold and certain. I had the thought that I should turn off the light, the room was already so flooded with afternoon sun, but I fell asleep before I could and didn't wake until I heard a shrill creak of the floorboard and the soft sound of my name.

"Honey," Bobbie said, a sliver of her face appeared in the crack between the door and frame. "They need to talk to you. Now."

I sat up, fully awake. I ran to the bedroom window, which looked out on Willow and Stefan's backyard and part of the driveway. If the police were here at the house then they had to be over at Stefan and Willow's, too.

I got there in time to see the children being led away to a minivan by a woman in sedate businesswear, a tidy bun.

Persephone came into the frame. She was held by the wrist and tugged to the woman's car by her assistant, a young man who attempted to crouch down and speak with her. She ignored him, reaching back and calling for someone out of my view. She held out one of her dolls, one with long, red hair. It fell on the ground at one point, but Sage picked it up and handed it to her. He was silent but wide-eyed, as though in shock, walking behind Persephone.

"Where's Mariah?" I asked, turning away from the window.

"You should come down," Bobbie said, "don't watch anymore. It's only going to make you feel worse."

I couldn't stop watching, especially when I saw Stefan come out, handcuffed. He was shouting and resisting. I could see that much, though I couldn't hear him, so I opened the window. Bobbie batted at my hands and said something about not doing it, not letting it upset me, but I wasn't paying attention to her anymore. I could hear Stefan now, if distantly. He was yelling something I couldn't make out. His long hair had been taken down and hung loose and shaggy around his shoulders. He was shirtless and wore a pair of sweatpants.

Shut the fuck up, I wanted to shout to him. He was making it all worse.

Willow came, next, her head hanging low. She was led away as though drugged, stumbling, though she raised her head when she saw the kids being ushered into the van. She shouted and her knees gave out, dropping her to the ground. The two police on either side of her had to hold her up, practically carrying her to the car.

"Where's Mariah?" I asked again.

"They took her away first," Bobbie said, gently shutting the window, snapping the metal locks in place. "They had to make sure she was safe before anything else. We'll get to talk to her soon. The detectives are downstairs waiting for you. You've got to tell them what you saw, though I think they saw the same thing as you did, not much confusion about it."

The officers motioned me to sit down across from them on the sofa.

I turned eighteen months ago, but they didn't see me as an adult, I could see that right away. They were correct to feel that way, because then, all I wanted to do was tell them that I took it back, that nothing had happened and that everything should go back to the way it was before.

"Are they okay? Are the kids okay?" I asked as soon as I sat down.

"We can't tell you about what's happening out there," one said. I can't remember what either of them looked like or their names, just the feeling of them, the practiced balance of distance and care. Techniques they'd probably been taught to put people at ease. He leaned forward to meet my eye. "But I can assure you that we're doing our best to make sure the children are safe, and Mariah, too. We just need to talk to you for a while. Then, you'll go down to the station and give your formal statement."

I told them what I'd seen, exactly. Bobbie sat next to me, holding my hand as I spoke.

"Did Mariah ever tell you about a sexual relationship between her and the couple?"

I shook my head. "I knew they were close, but she never said anything about a relationship."

"Did they ever ask you to do anything like this? To have any...inappropriate relations with them?"

I paused before I spoke. The sun was low in the sky, as it had been the night of the painting, which maybe they'd found, maybe they already knew. "No," I said. "They never did. They painted me and Mariah once, but it wasn't anything bad. We were covered up."

"I didn't know about that," Bobbie interrupted. She held my hand tighter.

"But the painting was no big deal. And they never touched me," I said. "They didn't make me do anything."

The officer leaned forward, interested now.

"What about anything else, something less obvious. Any suggestion to undress, to do something for them on video, anything that made you feel uncomfortable?"

I hesitated. Sometimes when Stefan touched me, it felt too close, but it was simply a feeling. And sometimes it was a feeling I wanted. I couldn't deny that, and I couldn't tell them.

"I'm eighteen," I said. "They didn't make me do anything."

Bobbie asked them if we could just talk down at the station. The car ride would do me good, she said, and they agreed, stating that a specialist in these kinds of cases would be there to talk to me and to Mariah, who was there already.

The police station was in a beige, strip-mall style building, a gloomy, wood-paneled space with buzzing lights. When we got there, they didn't take me to Mariah, but instead asked me to go into a smaller room, the walls empty, decorated only with a heavy, worn desk with a poster in Spanish that appeared to be about child abuse. There, we met a detective in plain clothes and a social worker. The detective was a young man, red-headed and freckled. The social worker, a middle aged woman with a clipboard. They made me go through the event again, in detail. I told them how I recognized Stefan's face. I told them about Willow's hair pulled back in a barrette the color of bone, catching her loose curls, and her chipped rose fingernail polish. I told them that I doubtless saw Mariah, my sister who I'd known for the entire fifteen years of her life. I told them about the painting, which had caused a furious burst of notes from the social worker.

And then, when I'd told it all, I begged them to not take away their kids.

"They love them," I said. "Whatever they did to Mariah, they never hurt them."

The social worker who they'd had sit next to me as I told my story reached out to touch my hand, which I'd unfolded and held upon in supplication. She was Bobbie's age, but somehow both abundant and prim, her round cheeks rouged, her matching skirt and jacket set institutional gray, though a soft pink turtleneck peeked up from the buttoned-up jacket.

When we finished questioning, I went out to the waiting room, where my aunt stood at one of the desks, a phone receiver to her ear. She mouthed the words *your mother's on the phone*.

I'd forgotten about Mom, who was the whole reason I'd found Mariah with them to begin with. I shook my head. Talking to her was the last thing I could imagine doing. I had a distant, pulsing memory of her hissing *then join her in the grave*. No room for that thought now, so I forced my mind to go black. Bobbie hung up soon after, telling Mom she'd let her know what happened next.

"Is she okay?" I asked. Mom being in the hospital had completely escaped my consciousness in the last four hours. At least she couldn't drink herself to death today, being in the hospital and all. Maybe it was for the best that she was there and not home.

Bobbie nodded. "Her bloodwork is stable, she'll be discharged as soon as tomorrow. She has to take her meds and start AA, that's the recommendation. She seems ready to start, at least now that this has happened. Maybe this will be the thing that gets her back into the world. Maybe one good thing could come out of it."

I wasn't ready to imagine a good thing happening from this, so I turned away and examined the bulletin board by the glass double doors, where notices about required permits crowded out yellowing posters with pictures of missing kids and teens. I wondered how many of them had been found, how many came back home on their own, how many ended up dead or unrecognizable, lost to a new, terrible life they had never intended to enter.

"It's my fault," Bobbie said, almost casually. She pressed

her lips together tight and looked away from me, up at the white ceiling, where a cluster of pencils hung, stuck up into the soft ceiling. "I should have watched you both better. I knew something was wrong with those two."

"No," I said. "Every time you asked me if something was wrong, I denied. it. Every time."

Bobbie pulled me in close to her. She didn't hug often, but when she did, it meant something. Her arms were weighty and strong. You didn't sink into a hug with Bobbie so much as feel wrapped up in it. "We're too good at keeping our mouths shut."

Bobbie breathed in deep and let the breath go.

"Let's end that today."

After another two hours, Mariah emerged from one of the witness rooms.

Her hair was disheveled, her face streaked with tears. She looked at me and her face twisted. When I say twisted, I mean it really seemed to change shape, to change essentially, her mouth like an animal twisting away from a source of pain.

"I won't go back with her," she said, pointing to me. "I won't be in the same house as her."

I didn't say anything. Bobbie, who was sitting next to me, grabbed my hand.

"Mariah," she began, "your sister — "

"She's not my sister anymore," Mariah said. "She ruined everything."

"We had to — "

"She was jealous," Mariah said. "They didn't like her and she wanted them to. She couldn't find a boyfriend, she couldn't even find a friend. And she was jealous of me, so she took them away, thinking she'd have me to herself, but she won't. Not ever again." Spit flew from her mouth as she spoke. The skin around her eyes was red, inflamed, and she held the back of a desk chair, her knuckles white. She wanted to hurt me. If we were alone in the room together, I wonder if she would have pounced on me like a cat.

I couldn't make my mouth move to say anything.

Bobbie shook her head, turning to me, then back to Mariah when she saw the blankness on my face. "Mariah, your sister loves you. I love you. This had to stop. It's not about jealousy, it's about your safety."

Mariah met my eye and I looked away. I had been jealous, that was true. Was that why I had told? I tried to remember back to a few hours ago, who I was then. No, what I'd felt was fear and disgust. I tried to hold onto that thought, even as Mariah kept looking at me with that new face, with a frightening blankness. I looked at her and knew it was pointless to say any of this aloud. We were both locked up inside ourselves and our different stories. I let myself leave the room, drift up to that brown-flecked ceiling.

I could hear Mariah continuing to argue with Bobbie: in the small waiting area, with only a half-dozen shabby, brown seats between us, there wasn't anywhere else to go. I heard her say that she wasn't going to go home with Bobbie if I was going to be there. She said she didn't want to live under the same roof as me, that she hated me. If I was going back to Mom, then she'd stay with Bobbie, if Bobbie would let her. If I was staying with Bobbie, then she'd be going with Mom.

"I don't care where I am," she said. "As long as I'm nowhere near her."

I couldn't listen to it anymore.

"Mariah," I shouted, drowning out her complaints. "I came to tell you that Mom's in the hospital. That's why I went over in the first place."

For a short moment, Mariah was back.

"What do you mean?" Mariah came closer, but still about six feet away.

"Hepatitis C, she's steady, she'll be out soon. She needs to stop drinking."

Mariah broke eye contact and then turned toward Bobbie.

"Am I allowed to stay at the hospital with Mom tonight? I want to get out of here as quick as I can."

Bobbie looked at me, then back at Mariah. "I don't think it's a good time for you to — "

"I won't stay with her." Mariah nodded toward me, but looked at Bobbie.

Bobbie rubbed her eyes and sighed.

"I'll take you over to see your mom and stay at the hospital for the night. After that, we're gonna go back to the house and clean up the place for your mother to come home. I'll be over there for a few weeks, helping her get settled back in, to get you settled in. Then, we'll talk."

"I'm fine by myself," Mariah said. She seemed young then, a kid in a dingy police station, the whole place grim with wood paneling and sickly yellow lights. I became aware that we weren't the only ones in the room, and everyone was watching us. Mariah followed my gaze. An elderly woman seated just a few feet away, her hands folded on her purse, looked on, as did the front desk officer, and two teenagers with their father, a heavily tattooed man with a cheek full of tobacco. He looked down at the floor.

Mariah let Bobbie lead her out, and a police officer delivered me back to the house alone.

I stood in the empty house, where everything had changed in just a few hours. I could still smell breakfast in the air. I hadn't eaten anything since then, and I didn't want to. I couldn't get myself to do anything but watch for activity over at Stefan and Willow's house, but the windows were dark, the lawn deep and green in the yellow streetlights. That night, I went directly to my room and got in bed and fell almost immediately asleep, a rarity for me, though I remember waking frequently throughout the night with the afterfeeling of a nightmare, though I couldn't remember what the nightmare had been. When I woke for good, it was day, and I smelled coffee and eggs. I sat up in bed and tried to imagine what the day would look like, what all the days would look like from now on. I called my work and told them I'd had a family emergency and to take me off of the schedule for the next two days. I looked out the window, where there was activity again at Willow and Stefan's house. Two police cars had parked on the driveway and on the lawn, right where Mariah and I had spun just a month and a half before, drunk and happier than we'd been since we were children.

I walked downstairs carefully, listening for the sounds of

conversation, but all I could hear was the radio, which Bobbie switched off when she saw me enter the dining room.

"I thought you were gonna stay with Mariah at the hospital?"

"I'll be over there again soon," she said. "I don't plan on just abandoning you here."

I shrugged, though I was grateful. I had thought she would abandon me. I was eighteen, after all, and not the victim of anything.

"You need to eat," she said. "No matter what you say, I'm gonna require that you eat."

I nodded. "I'm hungry, Bobbie. You don't have to convince me."

We ate in silence. I kept looking out the kitchen window, where I could see the back of the police cars, but nothing else.

"They've been over there since early," Bobbie said.

"No news, though?"

Bobbie shook her head. "It's all out of our hands now. We just wait."

"I hate this."

Bobbie nodded, then took a sip of coffee.

"Will Mariah come to get her things?"

Bobbie shook her head. "Not today. We're gonna find time to do that together."

"She doesn't want me here when she picks up her things."

Bobbie sighed. "She said she'd like to come get her things at a time when you were not here, yes. I told her I couldn't guarantee you wouldn't be here, since this is your home, but I said I'd let you know her preference."

"I won't make her see me," I said. "She hates me now. There's nothing I can do about it."

Bobbie set down her fork. "She doesn't hate you. She's angry for the moment, but she doesn't hate you. She'll come around."

"Then why do I feel like I did something wrong?"

The question hung in the air. I got up and scraped the remnants of my breakfast into the trash, then washed the dish clean, dried it, and put it back in the cabinet, all to make enough noise to distract myself from however Bobbie might answer that question.

"You feel bad because of how Mariah acted," Bobbie said. "But how she acted isn't about you, it's about her and what she felt when she was over there. What we saw at the station, that was how a child acts when something's been taken away from her. Surely you can see that?"

"Yeah, I can. But it doesn't matter. What matters is that she doesn't want me in her life, and without her, there's nobody... nobody holding me, nobody keeping me — "

I didn't know how to say what I wanted to say. There was nobody keeping me tethered to the world, nobody that made any of this matter.

"I'm sorry," she said. "You have a chance that she'll come back to you, if you don't push, if you give her time."

Bobbie's words sounded like wisdom, and they were wisdom, but they weren't truth. Truth and wisdom aren't the same thing. Nobody tells you that.

III

March 2017

I waited two weeks for Mariah's arrival. In those two weeks, information about The Family Circle reached the local news, then national. The local station aired the surveillance video, including Mariah, but named her as unidentified, and pleaded for somebody to give any names, anything they could possibly know about the blonde woman in her late twenties to early thirties. Then, the national news picked it up. Bobbie called me soon after the footage first aired.

"Did you see it?"

"Yeah."

"They know it's your sister, don't they?"

"Yes."

"I could tell it was her, too, just by her walk when they showed the video, even covered up with glasses and all that. She looks thin, doesn't she?"

"She does." Too thin.

"Why aren't they saying her name?"

I shrugged. "I bet they have a reason."

I waited days for them to say her name, but they never

did, and I was grateful for that. It made anything seem possible — maybe they'd never find her and she'd drift back into the darkness, living some strange, but safe life. This false sense of safety kept me going as I waited for her to arrive. Wheeler and Collier hadn't visited lately. I expected I wasn't a particularly useful source of information anymore since, as far as they knew, my sister had all but cut me out of her life. Bobbie called me and said they'd visited her, too.

"They asked me if I was harboring her somewhere in my house. I laughed out loud. Like this creaky place could hide anyone. I assured them I'd hadn't set eyes on Mariah in years and didn't expect to anytime soon."

Bobbie said they'd asked her about that summer, too, and that she told them everything she knew and some of what she'd heard later, too.

"I told them I think that summer changed her and that she never came back from it."

I remembered that morning after everything went wrong, when Bobbie had told me Mariah would realize I was just trying to take care of her, that she'd come back to me.

"Why didn't we ever get the old Mariah back?" I asked. "You said she'd come around, that we'd get her back some day. It didn't happen."

"I don't know. She must have been so much more lonely than we thought. You were becoming an adult and leaving. I wasn't much company and neither was your mother. She missed you so much on the days when you worked, before she started staying with them so much. She'd watch you leave and try to stay up until midnight so she could talk to you when you got home. You don't know how many times I had to wake her up from where she'd fallen asleep on the couch, just watching the window and waiting to see your little bike light coming from the distance."

I shook my head. "I don't remember that. I remember her being gone all the time."

"That wasn't until the end of July. In the beginning, it was you I was worried about."

"Why me?"

"You were preoccupied with this boy at work. I was worried you'd get distracted from school, that you'd end up, well, like your mother. Pregnant, miserable, looking at the rest of your life as a slog to get through. You were drinking a lot, too."

I was shocked into momentary silence. I didn't think Bobbie knew the extent of our drinking. I didn't think I had been preoccupied with anyone, at least not openly. I thought I'd been hiding so well.

"That's right," she said, as though hearing my thoughts. "I'm no dummy."

"We thought you'd just decided to clean it out." Of course, saying this aloud revealed how silly it was. Bobbie didn't simply decide to do things that didn't need to be done.

"And you were leaving us all soon, going off to college. You were already gone by the end."

"I wasn't really leaving," I said. "I wasn't ever going to leave her. I wanted her to come live with me in an apartment. I was planning on working instead of going to community college, even."

It was Bobbie's turn for silence. "Honey, you never told her that, not me, either. And if you'd told me that plan, or her, we would have talked you out of it. You were going off in your own direction, as you always were going to do. You weren't ever going to stick around."

I blinked, angry as well as hurt. "I would have stayed with her. There at the end, I planned to abandon everything to take care of Mom. You don't know what I was planning."

Bobbie sighed. "I don't doubt you were or that you had it in your head to take care of her when your mom got sick. My point is that Mariah could tell you were pulling away, beginning to carve out a new life. And that was absolutely right for you to do. It isn't your fault what happened to Mariah. I wish I could tell you something that makes sense and explains it. All I know is that more happened than we know between her and Stefan and Willow. For some reason, she couldn't shake the idea that they were her real family."

"Maybe we weren't good enough."

Bobbie didn't try to argue. "Maybe we weren't. But we tried. We did our best. We gave her space to come back, but she didn't."

"How do you deal with it? How do you not feel guilty?" I was peeling the wallpaper again, getting old glue and paper stuck beneath my nails.

"I used to feel guilty all the time, but I couldn't keep feeling that way. When I think back, when I try to put myself back there, I know I did what I could with the information I had. I messed up in allowing her over there so much, in ignoring some of the red flags. I could have done better, but what I remember, what I want you to remember, is that we didn't do this. They did."

When Mariah finally came, I was nursing Faun at the kitchen table, nervously watching the egg timer, which I suspected would go off before the baby was ready. I'd have to pull her off before she was done, which meant she'd start screaming, or worse, bite my nipple to keep me from unlatching her little sucker mouth. I considered just letting the timer go off until she let me go, allowing the eggs to boil into inedible dust. Then, Watson stood up and ran to the back window, barking wildly.

I didn't hear a car, and there was no entrance from the backyard. I figured the dog was barking at some wild animal, but the way he came to me bouncing with excitement, and then back to the living room windows, hurling himself at the glass, was exactly how he told me somebody was coming down the road. When I went to the window, I saw a figure coming through the backyard, a woman in winter clothes. The only way they could have come was through the woods, which as far as I knew, stretched out beyond to nowhere, hitching up to the Adirondacks at some point in the distance where they rose in soft, blue and green hills. She wore a puffy black jacket and a hat, as well as sunglasses. She was overdressed for the weather, which was snowy but sunny, and I imagined she was sweating beneath all that disguise.

Mariah.

I unlatched the baby and jiggled her until she stopped crying. For once, she complied, and almost immediately began to blink slowly, her head on my shoulder.

Seeing Mariah coming toward me was like looking forward to a date with a person you'd dreamed about for years and never imagined you could have. I looked down at my clothes, a t-shirt I'd thrown on a few days ago and never gotten around to changing and a pair of Colin's sweatpants. It had been so long since I'd seen Mariah that I wondered if she'd recognize me, and if she recognized me, would she be disappointed by how much I had changed? I was stringy-haired and hadn't had a bath for days except a half-hearted splash of water on my face and armpits. She'd chosen to come during the day, while Colin was at work, so I hadn't gotten a chance to properly dress myself for dinner. I at least tried to wear a clean shirt for that.

I looked around the room for a brush, a different shirt, anything to make myself feel put together.

2000 to 2004

When I lived with Bobbie, after it was clear Mariah was never coming back, I fell into what I think of as my lost years. Maybe thinking of it that way is wrong — I wasn't lost so much as unmoored. The way I had imagined my life since I was a kid was no longer possible. I had assumed I'd go to college eventually, that Mariah would come along with me, that we'd go back to Mom's every once in a while and help her out, maybe buy her a new house in her old age. Now, I had to figure out who I was without those vague plans propelling me forward.

I went back to work at the restaurant and I got back together with Jackson. What I mean by that is that I cornered him after work about a week after Stefan and Willow were arrested and kissed him against the wall behind the restaurant, pressing him so hard he had to push me off his chest.

"Do you still want to, you know, talk sometimes?" I asked, finding myself just as pathetic as he must have seen me.

I could see some fear in his eyes, so I stepped back completely, giving him space.

"I don't want anything of you," I said. "I just want things

to be like they were before I got mad. I get it. It's hard to be alone, and we don't have to be."

Jackson nodded. "I, I kept meaning to call you. I heard about the stuff with your sister. I'm sorry about what happened. I don't know a whole lot about it, but I bet it's hard."

I froze up. People at work had heard about Willow and Stefan, who I had spoken about often, and even if they didn't know exactly what had happened, they could tell by context clues that Mariah must be involved. I'd even had a few sympathetic words from co-workers. Most townies had a police radio — it was considered an entertainment must in a town where most of the entertainment cleared out October through April. One co-worker had tried to pull me in for a hug, which I had endured stiffly. Most people hadn't said much of anything about it, though, whether out of politeness or a lack of interest or blissful unawareness of the local news, I wasn't sure and didn't care to know.

"It's okay," I said. "It's not something I like talking about. I'm just trying to forget about it, to be honest."

He shrugged. "I get it."

I was beginning to think that my tertiary involvement with a salacious crime was ruining my change of having a friend-with-benefits situation with Jackson. Then, he stepped forward and tipped my chin up.

"I'd like to hang out tonight," he said. "You wanna smoke?"

"Yeah," I said.

And so we started things up again, and this time, he asked me questions, too. It was mostly about my sister and what had happened to her, what had happened with Stefan and Willow. I hadn't wanted to talk about it at first, but eventually, I warmed up to it. Talking to somebody else about what had happened made it feel real and solid. I was going to have to give testimony, but that would come later: the law moved very slowly, not like on TV. Not speaking made me fear I'd forget it all, and I didn't want to forget — I'd carry the whole thing with me like a heavy backpack, I felt I had to, it was my punishment. So I practiced with Jackson, telling him all the little details of those first dinners, but I stopped short when it came to that last day.

"I don't want to talk about that," I told him. This new interest in me had paid off by giving me some power in the relationship. I could tell him to fuck off and not think he was going to leave me because I truly didn't care, and my not caring was interesting to him. He liked me now because I was tragic. As long as I could supply him with some unusual sadness, he'd want me.

I didn't tell Bobbie about this relationship, which lasted, in fits and starts, for far longer than it should have. We kept it up even after I started at the community college that Spring, and after I went to the state school thirty minutes away. And, to my shame, we continued even after Jackson and his Dunkin Donuts girlfriend got engaged. It only ended after he moved to Boston for a writing degree, where he brought his fiancée, and then wife, and disappeared, at least to me. He sent me one of his stories once, a few years after he got married. He'd published it in a literary magazine with a glued-on cover, the words running into the ditch of the page, making each last word in the sentence nearly unreadable. He had sent the story with a sticky note attached, saying I'd been the inspiration for this one. The story was about a man, a writer, who spent his days struggling to finish a novel and his nights with a mysterious woman who refused to speak to him. She'd only gesture, leading him to her bedroom, sleep with him, and then cry inconsolably into his arms until they both fell asleep. I didn't finish the story, annoyed by the narrator, by my supposed role as a muse for this story about a woman who doesn't speak, who is quite literally an empty place for the narrator to throw meaning. I had never cried into his arms. I'd done exactly the opposite, talking all night and usually leaving right after sex. He had been the empty place where I'd thrown my story, that's how I wanted to think of it, though I suppose we both needed to project something onto each other, some way to feel powerful.

During this time, I also started up the affair with my history professor. I was aware of the limitations of the relationship: that's what I liked about it. I didn't really want a relationship. Willow and Stefan had been in a relationship. Bobbie and Cassandra had been in a relationship. I wasn't foolish. I knew that not every happy family was dark beneath the surface, not every person you love will die young, but something about happiness had been soured for me. It was hard to believe two people could create it together.

March, 2017

Mariah refused my offer to take her jacket.

"I won't be here long," she said. She looked nervously around the house, insisting on opening every door to check for anybody else nearby — the one to Faun's room, my bedroom, and the laundry room, as well as the basement, which she asked to search thoroughly, though I told her I hadn't been down there in months and didn't know the state of things. She used my phone flashlight to make her way down, but the unfinished depths of it, crowded with Colin's things and spiderwebs and an oppressive, moldy smell, convinced her that nobody was hiding out.

"I haven't told anyone," I said after she emerged from the dark entrance, pulling strands of web from her hair. "If that's what you're worried about. And Colin won't be home until five."

"I believe you," she said. "I just don't trust them."

"Who?"

"The FBI. For all you know, somebody could have been here without your knowledge."

"I doubt that," I said. "I never leave this place."

I led her to the kitchen table. The baby cried out; I'd been holding her too tight. I shifted her around so she faced forward, looking out onto the world.

Mariah smiled. "Faun," she said. "I'm so glad I got to meet her. I like that name. It's otherworldly."

I paused, remembering when Mariah had been described as otherworldly by Stefan.

"Do you want to hold her?" Mariah initially raised her arms, then lowered them, looking down at her jacket.

"Please," I said. "Take her. She loves new people."

This was true — sometimes Faun seemed to love new people more than she loved me, settling down in their arms as though finally finding a safe place to rest. Of course, I had also once been worried that she loved the ceiling fan more than me, she'd been so enthralled by the moving blades.

Mariah sighed and then held out her arms again and took her. Faun rested on the shoulder of Mariah's puffy jacket, pulling at the fabric, fascinated by the sound it made.

This was how it was always supposed to be, me and Mariah. This was the old plan.

"Stay with us," I said, knowing it was too soon, that I'd blow the moment. "Just stay. Whatever they've got, it can't be better than family."

Mariah shook her head. "It's too late," she said. "You've gotta know by now I can't just stop. They've contacted you, so they've probably bugged this place. They're probably getting all of your calls. They probably put a tracker on your car so that when you left, they came and set up all the surveillance. They are probably watching us right now." Mariah didn't seem particularly bothered by this, but my stomach dropped. I felt like an idiot. Of course they knew. I could only blame my distracted mind, the deadening repetition of taking care of a baby, for making me think I had any privacy as the closest living relative of somebody wanted by the FBI.

"I'm so sorry," I said. "I didn't realize…"

"It's okay. I knew the risk, and I know you didn't mean to harm me. I believe you when you say you didn't tell them."

I closed my eyes and nodded, not able to meet her eye. I would continue to lie to her about contacting them. I couldn't see the value in telling her now, and I don't regret it, still. I want to hold onto this last meeting as it was, with her believing that I hadn't talked.

Mariah kissed Faun gently on the head and handed her back to me.

I was having a hard time paying attention to Mariah's words — I was marveling at how much she had changed. Her eyes were lined with wrinkles, her lips chapped from the cold, her cheeks, too, sore and red, which should have made her look youthful, but instead, she simply looked windburned and exhausted, her under eyes blue. She had taken off her cap, at least, and set it on the table. Her hair, her beautiful hair, was greasy and flat. She'd cut it short, around her ears, and had slicked it all back for maximum utility. Mariah had never been interested in makeup and was never terribly vain, but she'd always had a…look. She liked her skin to be fresh and clear, her clothes loose and preferably covered in flowers. Now, everything she wore was utilitarian, her jacket enormous, her pants puddling around her boots. She looked to have lost twenty pounds that she couldn't stand to lose, always having been slight and willowy. Despite her puffy jacket, I could see her hands, how bony they were, and how the chords of her throat stood out when she spoke.

I wanted to feed her, and hug her, but I couldn't yet. I had to know why she was really here.

"Why are they after you?" I asked. "They said something about bombings and The Family Circle. Do you know what they're talking about?"

Mariah shook her head and smiled down at her emaciated hands, as though she felt sorry for me, for my ignorance.

"We've never hurt anyone who did not do something that called for it." Her voice flat, unreal. The kind of voice you use when you are trying to reveal nothing.

"What the fuck does that mean?"

She tugged the sleeve of her coat down over her hands. "You wouldn't understand."

"You're right. I don't understand. Tell me you weren't part of it," I said. "That you didn't know what was going to happen."

"I can't tell you that," she said. This was sharp, clear, with no apology. "I knew what was happening and why. I even helped with bomb construction." She looked around the room, laughing. "For whoever is listening, yeah, I did it. I knew the targets. It was all my choice."

I had almost forgotten the baby in my arms. I'd been rocking gently, robotically, and she had fallen asleep, her tiny eyelashes resting against her perfect cheek. It hit me then, as it sometimes did, that we've all been babies. Mariah had been a baby once, as had I. We'd been vulnerable and soft and wanted nothing but love. I had to remind myself of this even as I wanted to scream in her face that she was a fucking idiot who would ruin her life to live like this, bone thin and wearing rags she'd probably found in a free box at a church rummage sale, nothing in her life but this group that had apparently encouraged her to come here, to me, and announce her guilt.

I let the baby sleep in my arms because I couldn't bear to leave the room and run the risk that I might come back to find Mariah gone again.

"I don't want to hear this," I said, finding some composure. "This isn't you."

Mariah nodded. "I would have said the same thing years ago. I never would have imagined myself here. But here I am, waiting for the FBI to show up, having assembled bombs that killed one woman and injured others."

She was saying this on purpose.

"Listen, Mariah, they told me they're willing to work with you if you come forward, if you reveal who Agape is. They told me they could offer you a reduced sentence."

For just a moment, I thought I could see her considering it, see her imagining a life beyond this moment, but then she became opaque to me again and smiled.

"A reduced sentence. How generous. But somehow I don't think it's going to matter much. They're gonna figure out who Agape is no matter what I do."

"But if you tell them now, maybe you'll get out soon."

"I did what I did for a reason, Chelsea. If I did that, none of it would mean anything."

"But why did you do it?" I asked. "What was it supposed to mean? Did this guy, this Agape guy, make you do these things?"

"He wasn't the only reason — I wanted to right a wrong. I wanted to give justice that the world wouldn't give."

I shook my head, trying to make sense of what she was saying. "How was it justice, Mariah? A fucking social worker? What good did it do?"

"We have a plan. We spent time in hiding, but now we're no longer hiding." Her clarity was back, that fierce, clear look in her eye that said she was certain and I was a fool.

"Maybe you should have hidden a bit better so we wouldn't end up here in my kitchen, waiting for the police to arrive."

Mariah smiled. "Chelsea, you've always been so caught up in this illusion, in the pain of the 3-D world. You get all tangled up and can't see yourself anymore. We were always going to end up here. What's happening right now was always going to happen and has happened before, over and over again. We are exactly where we need to be."

I felt the old helplessness of Mariah pulling down the curtain and turning away. My arms ached from Faun's weight. I had to leave. Needed to leave.

"I'm going to put the baby down," I said, seizing the opportunity to step away from the table and collect myself. "Don't go anywhere, please."

As I placed Faun in the crib, I tried to prepare myself to respond. I was angry. I began to shake and realized that what I wanted to do most was slap Mariah in the face. I also wanted to crawl into the blankets with her and watch a movie like we used to. I told myself that I had to stay in the room and do neither of those things. I breathed in deep until my hands stopped shaking. I walked back out and put a kettle on the stove. Then, I sat across from her, placing both my hands on the table before me.

"I am tired of this," I said. "What you said about me being stuck in illusions — you say shit like that all the time. I won't be your punching bag anymore. Whatever belief you have about what happened that summer, however you see it, you know that I did what I did because I wanted you safe. Because I love you. And the fact that you won't admit it, that you keep me at a distance, that you pretend your fucked up life is going a whole lot better than my fucked up life, that's some bullshit that I won't take from you anymore."

The kettle whistled its shrill music and shook gently against the red coils. Mariah whispered. "The water's ready."

I stood up and made two cups of tea, dunking the bags into two plain, white mugs, the kind you get at a diner. Mariah and I both loved diner cups. Coffee tastes better out of a thick, white diner mug. The tea darkened and I removed the bags, squeezing out some of the water.

"Honey?" I asked.

"Yeah," she said.

I placed the steaming cup before her.

"I know I haven't been fair to you." She said. Mariah was back. She put her hair behind her ears and a hank fell back, obscuring her face. Another fell again, and I was reminded of when I gave her a terrible bob that constantly escaped from behind her ears, she must have been thirteen. "I've been thinking about it for a long time lately, how much I blamed you for what happened."

"Then why do you keep doing it? Why are you still so angry with me?"

She shook her head. "I know you didn't mean it, but you didn't just hurt me, you hurt them, too. You ruined their lives."

"They deserved to have their lives ruined."

She shook her head, close to tears. "They lost their children, Chelsea. They spent time in prison. You don't know how far it rippled, how much they lost. And by the time they got out — "

She stopped short.

Oh Christ, I thought. She's in contact with them. And then it hit me, what I should have realized right away, that man wrapped in scarves, unrecognizable at first, and then I remembered the loping, lazy movement of him that I watched from a distance when he was playing in the yard with the kids or coming toward me in that warm house, always smelling of oranges and wine and something wonderful cooking, his arms held out for an embrace.

"It's Stefan. He's Agape."

She paused, leaned back, her eyes closed, and nodded. "I'm not hiding anything anymore, there's no point. I know they're listening, but it's okay. He's not trying to escape, he did what he needed to do and he's done. I'm done, too."

The FBI probably suspected it, which was why they had asked me about that summer in such detail. They'd hidden this detail from me.

"He made you send those bombs for him. He's doing it again."

Mariah laughed out loud. "You have always underestimated me, Chelsea. Nobody makes me do anything. That's what I told you back then, and it's always been true. It was my idea."

I had looked up the victims of the bombings in the last week, since their names were released and connected to The Family Circle. One woman, who had sustained serious injuries and was still in critical condition, was a former social worker who had recently retired from her work with the Massachusetts Department of Human Services. Another was a housewife who had, over the years, fostered twelve children. She'd later died of her injuries. Next was a former attorney who now worked for a nonprofit that exonerated people who had been convicted of crimes they did not commit. The crimes had been baffling — these were people who had given their lives to public service to taking care of children.

Now it was clear. They had something to do with Willow and Stefan's children.

Mariah yawned. She seemed deeply tired and it occurred to me that they were probably on their way now to arrest her. Maybe this was the last time I'd see her free. We couldn't squander this time fighting about the past.

"Why did you come here, if there's no hope, if nothing can change and you won't come home?"

Mariah looked up at me, eyes red. "I wish we could," she said. "I wish we could go back to the way things were. I wish I could stay here with you and the baby. I've just gone so far, there's nothing else I can do. I can't convince you that they didn't do anything wrong. I can't convince you that the law is wrong. I can just say that after that summer, I was never happy the same way again. I never felt free the same way again."

"Mariah, they didn't care for you. They were reckless. They were abusive. They treated you like they treated all the others. If you'd stuck around long enough, they would have abandoned you, too."

It was so difficult to get out of this ugly groove, to not think that I could steer her toward seeing clearly if I just said it the right way. We'd been having the same senseless conversation for over fifteen years.

Mariah didn't appear to get angry. She stirred her tea, seeming to consider my words. As far as I remembered, she'd never done this before.

"I don't believe that's true, that they didn't care about me. I don't think you understand. It wasn't sex, that wasn't the important part for me. They loved me, like every part of me. We had a family, but it was better than a regular family: I was chosen. That's why losing them was such a blow."

I felt a great weariness: how could I contradict this? These were her feelings; I didn't have a way to change them. So I stopped. Finally, I stopped.

"How long have you been in contact with Stefan?"

She brightened at this question, which felt like a punch to the chest, but I tried not to show it. "About five years. Well, even before that, I wrote him, and Willow, too, when they were in prison."

"Why didn't you tell me?"

It was a stupid question, so I let the words die in the air.

"I don't think you understand how lonely I've been."

"I would have been there for you if you'd — "

She held her hand up. "Just let me talk. I'm not like you, Chelsea. I need people."

I winced inwardly at this, but tried not to show it. I was practicing listening to her. Maybe I hadn't been doing that for years.

"All you need are a couple of people, like Colin and the baby. But I was always looking for a different kind of family — I want to find my people. When I lost Willow and Stefan, I lost everything. I lost you as well as them. I was left with Mom, and since you never came over anymore, you never saw how it was toward the end."

I had stayed away because of Mariah, but I had to admit, not seeing my mother had been an unexpected benefit of our rift. She had never made good on her promise to stop drinking, so things just got worse and worse until her body gave out. I'd never had to clean her up after she pissed her bed or threw up in the bathroom, she didn't get to that point until well into my college career. I hadn't watched her whittle herself down to a loose-skinned, skeletal nightmare, a swirl of cigarette smoke and vodka fumes. I saw her on holidays, noted the change, spoke sadly about it to my friends and Bobbie, and then, I left. I had not had to identify her body — by then, I'd put enough distance between myself and my home that nobody expected me to show up for anything but the funeral. Mariah had done all of that.

"I was so alone then," Mariah said. "I wanted to call you all the time."

"Why didn't you?"

She shrugged. "I was angry with you."

"I was angry with you, too. I thought you hated me."

Mariah shook her head. "Of course I hated you! But later, I hated you for staying away. It started to seem like you didn't care. You didn't fight for me, Chelsea. I was waiting for you to come and help me, to notice I was lonely, but you didn't come. You left me alone."

She wasn't making sense. "I didn't leave you alone. You ignored me. You avoided me. I couldn't exactly force you to have a relationship with me."

Mariah's voice rose. "How could I talk to you? You were never around. You never reached out. I thought you were…I thought you were disgusted by me. That if you thought they were perverted or wrong, then I was, too."

All I could do was open my mouth, then close it, too baffled for the words to come. She had wanted me to come to her. She had wanted me to fight for her. The idea was astounding. I wasn't a fighter. I had let relationships, jobs, and places fall away from me as easily as you let your tight clothes fall away when you get home from work. I had the idea that if somebody left, then it would be rude to follow them, rude to impose myself where I wasn't wanted. I've let so many people go.

Oh, but I knew this, too: Mariah liked to be embraced, to be wooed by the world. Of course she wanted me to come to her and invite her back in.

"I didn't know. I didn't understand what you needed."

She reached her hand across the table and covered mine, where I was digging my nails into the wood.

"We both fucked up. We were young and stupid and had nobody looking out for us. Mom couldn't do it. And let's be real, as much as we both love Bobbie, she's not the person you go to for advice about how to be more, I dunno, emotionally real."

I took a chance and turned my hand around, palm up, and held her hand.

"You're right," I said. "We're quite a pair, aren't we? I don't blame you. All these years, I've blamed myself. I know I fucked it up. I know why you hate me. But Mariah, what else could I do?"

She shook her head. "It's okay, Chelsea. We don't have to do this. It's too late — "

"I felt so guilty for so long," I continued, waving her words away. I had to say it. "Sometimes I wish I hadn't said anything, Mariah, but I couldn't keep it in."

She took my hands in both of hers, holding me steady until the wave passed. We were vibrating together now, as though we were on the same frequency of sadness, finally.

"I saw them with you and I knew," I said. "I knew it in a way that wasn't even words, it was just on the gut level — it was wrong, and I couldn't let it happen to you anymore. Do you understand? Did you ever feel even a little bit like that?"

Mariah let go of my hands, but not as a gesture of rejection. She was looking down at the table, blinking. She had teared up and didn't want me to see.

"Sometimes I think about Willow. I wanted her to be like

my mom," she said. "Sometimes I wondered why she didn't stop it, slow it down, why it wasn't good enough for me to be her child, and her to be like my mom." She sniffled, rubbing her nose with the rough, noisy fabric of her coat.

I nodded. "I think I didn't ask you more, I didn't feel as worried as I should have, because I thought that surely Willow would protect you. Surely she wouldn't let anything bad happen if she was around."

I remembered that night when I went to Willow, after that terrible phone call with my mother. I'd trusted her after that.

We made eye contact and held it.

"I'm sorry," I said. "I'm sorry for everything."

"I'm sorry, too," she said.

"Tell me about you and Stefan writing to each other." If she'd been talking to him for years, I needed to understand why. Mariah said she was beyond saving, beyond change, but I couldn't accept that.

"It wasn't just Stefan, but Willow, too. We wrote near-weekly for the six years they were in prison. When they got out, they got back together, but they didn't come to see me until two years ago, when they joined The Family Circle."

"You lived with them."

Mariah nodded.

"And that's why you've barely called and visited for so long."

"By then, Willow was already dying of breast cancer," Mariah said. "She was diagnosed soon after she was released from prison. She was so hopeful at first, and so happy to see me.

Chelsea, it was like having a mom again. She had this beautiful gray hair — she'd aged a great deal in the last ten years, but she was still herself, still so elegant. She had a mastectomy and then chemotherapy and then radiation. She was in remission for a year until they found it had traveled to her lymph nodes. Six months later she was gone."

"I nursed her most days. By then, Stefan had become an organizer in The Family Circle and we were doing the daily meditation and lectures for the upstate New York chapter."

"He'd become a leader."

She shook her head. "We don't have leaders. He got interested in it because it was one of the one places where a person with a record could feel like a human again. Do you know how difficult it is for a person on the sex offender registry to get a job, to get a house? It's nearly impossible without family, and he lost his family when he was convicted."

I didn't argue, though I wanted to. "I wish you'd told me some of this. I wish I'd even had a clue."

"A few times I called you with them right there in the room. I wondered if you could feel anything different from those calls."

I shook my head. I had felt nothing but a desperate desire to make Mariah really, truly talk to me.

"And so Stefan decided to get back at the people who had ruined his life?" I asked. "That's what this was about?"

Mariah shrugged. "I think it was bigger than just him. He cared about injustice. This was meant to send a message."

I didn't bother to point out that if he cared about injustice, he could have devoted his life to dozens of things, but instead he'd spent his time out of prison planning to kill the people who had taken care of his children when he was unable to. I am glad I didn't say this, even if it was the truth. I'm glad I was able to keep her in the room with me for this long, at least.

Watson had started to pace around the room and bark, as he often did right before Colin came home from work. I called him over and tried to soothe him, but he would not be calmed. It was an hour before Colin was supposed to be back. I hoped he wasn't sensing a car coming, a whole fleet of cars, maybe. I hoped he was just anxious, or that maybe Colin was about to be home early.

The dog broke away from my hold and went to the door, then back to me, his little nails clicking against the floor, back and forth, evading me each time.

"I wish I could have kept you safe," I said.

"We did keep each other safe for a while. Until that summer."

I nodded. The tears came up, but I didn't try to hide them. "We did, didn't we?"

Watson began to bark and scratch at the door.

"Maybe he's got to use the bathroom," I said, hopeful but knowing that wasn't it. "Let me take him out and see."

"Wait a minute," she held out her hand and grabbed me before I made it to the door. "They know I'm here, you've got to know that."

I nodded.

"The dog's nervous because somebody's coming," Mariah

said. "They'll be here soon."

My mouth was dry. "Just leave. Run out the back and into the woods to where you came from."

"I parked my car as far out as I could, but they've found it by now. I didn't come here to run away, I came to talk to the police."

I felt hope for the first time that night. She was going to end it. She would be okay.

"Okay," I said. "That's good. I think turning yourself in is a good idea."

Mariah looked down at her jacket, fidgeting with the buttons. "I feel silly now," she said. "I don't feel so sure of everything as I did when I first started walking through the woods to your house. I don't feel so sure about what I know I need to do."

"Why?"

She shook her head and didn't answer. "I just need you to promise me something," she said. "When I step out there, keep the baby and dog in the back room and don't come out with me."

"I'm not gonna let you — "

"You have to listen to me. You can't come out. I don't want you to be there to see it. I won't be able to do this if you don't let me do it alone. I don't want you to see me like that, handcuffed and stuffed into a cop car. I want us to say goodbye here."

I tried to protest, but she clutched my arm even harder. "I am serious. Do not come out there. Let me choose how to turn myself in. Let me make this one, right choice, okay?"

I nodded. "So this is goodbye, then. At least for a little while."

She smiled. "It's goodbye."

"I'll write you, okay? I'll visit. You have a home here when you get out. Hell, I'll sell this house to pay for a lawyer who can get you off completely."

I didn't know what the hell I was talking about.

"Shhh," Mariah said, taking both of my hands in hers. "I love you."

"I love you, too."

"Go back there with the baby and the dog, now. Shut the door. "

I called Watson to me and with one last look back toward the door, he came forward, looking up at Mariah, too. She reached down her hand and caressed him between his ears, which he allowed her to do, though not for long.

She waited to step outside until she saw me go into the back room and shut the door behind me.

I went to Faun, who greeted me with wails of hunger.

"Sweet Faun," I whispered, as I heard the sound of cars rolling up the noisy driveway. "Shhhhhhh" I said, rocking her gently. Watson began to whine and then bark, that howling warning bark that was meant to tell me that something unusual was happening, something I should see. I heard the distant sound of shouts, which soon became frantic, and my heart began to beat fast. Faun cried out, responding to my fear. I tried to hush her as I moved toward the door. I knew Mariah had told me not to leave the room, but I couldn't help it: I needed to know.

I opened the door just as the windows by the front door blew inward, exploding in their frames from the outside. The sound was deafening, it rocked the house. The baby made a quick, sharp squeal, and when I looked down into her face, I saw a dark streak across her cheek, then the cut bloomed little globules of blood. Glass from the windows. My hands, too, were patterned with little pieces of glass. The dog howled and retreated back into the room, shivering in the corner, pawing at his left eye, shaking his head. I felt warmth on my own face and reached up to touch it. Blood. I didn't realize until later, but a chunk of glass had slit my scalp deep enough to require stitches. It sent a curtain of blood down my face, though at the time I didn't know how deep it was or how much I was bleeding.

Seeing Faun's blood threw me into a panic. I couldn't keep my feet and instead sank down to the floor, cradling Faun, checking her body for glass. Soon, my phone began to ring from the kitchen, and after it went silent, it rang again, and again. I was afraid to move, afraid of another enormous rumble that would break more of my house to pieces, but I eventually set Faun back into her crib and crawled to where it had scooted around and fallen from the kitchen table, the screen cracked but still visible, and called the number back.

It was detective Collier. "Chelsea, are you inside the house?"

"Yes, me and the baby and the dog."

"Okay," she said. "I need you to stay put, okay? Did you know that Mariah had the explosives?"

"What explosives?"

"Under her jacket. When she stepped out, she unzipped her jacket and detonated an explosive. I need to know if you were aware of this when she stepped out."

"No, Christ, no. Is she okay?"

Collier ignored the question. "Was she ever alone in a room without you? Could she have had access to any part of your house without you present?"

I shook my head, then remembered that she couldn't see me and that I'd have to speak.

"No. Well, just thirty seconds, when I put the baby down to sleep. That's the only time."

Collier seemed impatient with me. "That's enough time for her to have planted something. You're gonna have to wait inside the baby's room until the bomb squad comes to make sure she hasn't left us anymore surprises. Wait there, and stay put with the dog and baby. Stay low, preferably behind any larger furniture. Try to keep the dog calm. Officers will be inside to escort you out as soon as it's deemed safe, but it's going to be alarming, they are gonna be in full gear. Try to keep the dog from attacking; if you've got a leash, that's the best bet. Do what they say and everything will be all right."

"Is Mariah okay?"

She hung up.

March/April/May 2017

  I didn't return to the house for a long time. Because it was a crime scene, the state had to comb the area for bomb fragments and possible bombs planted elsewhere. They collected the pieces, both of the explosive and Mariah's body. After they were done with the evidence, they allowed us to cremate her and take the ashes. I did not have to identify her body; there was very little left to identify. They simply let me look at two pieces of jewelry that she'd been wearing: a simple ring that she'd worn since she was teenager and a cursive pendant of the letter "M," an almost girlish piece of costume jewelry that I now wear around my own throat.

  The officers had eventually come through the front door in full gear, tearing apart the kitchen, searching through the cabinets and under the tables, kicking over the trash can and opening every drawer. I watched them destroy the house through a crack in the door. Then, they came back to the room, their faces obscured with masks. The baby screamed when they came in. They had to shout through the gear in order for us to hear them. I held the dog back, though he snapped, his body stiff, and he nearly bit me as I struggled to hold both him and the howling baby. He'd been pacing as the officers ransacked the room, pawing at the walls until he tore the wallpaper away. He shit on the floor and howled in agony that he couldn't protect us from whatever was happening outside, all the terrible sounds and anxiety rippling through the air, through me. They led us through the backdoor and then around, past a temporary barricade that was put up to block the bomb site. There might have been scattered pieces of detritus on the ground, there might have been blood, but I couldn't see it. I kept my focus on moving forward, the baby in my arms, and the dog, held tightly against me on the short leash, following the back of an armored man.

When we emerged from the barricades, Colin was there, running for us as soon as we were in sight.

"We need a paramedic over here, now," the officer shouted, and from the smoke and gloom of the darkening winter evening, EMTs rushed over with a white, white bed, where they asked me to lie down and attended to my wounds.

Colin was by my side, holding me close. "I don't even understand what happened," I told Colin, handing him the baby and the leash so I could sit. The dog was thoroughly terrified, his tail between his legs. He whined until Colin held out a hand and let him lick it.

"I came up just in time to see her come out the door," he said. He was shaken, I had the sense that he wanted to tell me something terrible, something that would stay with me, that I wouldn't be able to undo, because it was too much for him to hold on his own. Fortunately, Detective Collier stepped forward and ordered Colin to call a family member who could come take the baby and dog so we could head to the police station and give statements after my injuries were taken care of.

"I am so sorry," he said, after calling his mother. "She's gone, Chelsea."

Hearing him say it was almost a relief. "I know."

We lived in the hotel for several months. For the first week, Colin took over the responsibilities for Faun while I stayed in bed, staring up at the ceiling fan for hours, listening to the same rotations of albums on my headphones. Nick Drake, Gene Clark, and Etta James. Back in the summer of 1999, Willow had called them her sad angels.

In the days after, Detective Collier came with her condolences and a list of crime scene cleanup companies that were willing to come out to the country.

"I am so sorry it happened this way, Chelsea. None of us wanted this."

I doubted she cared about Mariah beyond her ability to track down Agape, but I simply nodded. I still wasn't sure exactly what *this* was. Mariah had come to my house with explosives strapped to her body. She had never intended to leave alive. Maybe she'd never intended for me to leave alive, either.

"Thanks," I finally mustered.

Collier remained in the doorway, then pointed to the paisley-patterned chair in the corner, by the standard-issue hotel desk piled with baby supplies. I nodded.

"I'll take Faun for a walk around the hallway," Colin said,

and left me in the room with Collier.

She sat down on the hard-backed hotel chair. I sat on the queen-sized bed, on the already-stained white bedspread, so thin you could see right through it to the yellow sheet beneath. Above our bed, a clumsy watercolor of a mountainside, a waterfall vomiting from the peak down into a murky pool, took up an alarming amount of space. It crowded out the accent wall, painted a muted rose. I liked the ugly anonymity of this room. It was an empty space to absorb all the confusion in my head. I could stare at that improbable waterfall and where it dropped into some dark emptiness and feel something like peace.

"So, you've finished looking for whatever you were looking for and now we can go home?" I asked.

"We weren't looking for anything in particular. We wanted to make sure they hadn't planted anything around your house or left any other evidence that could point us to Agape."

"You know it's Stefan, right?"

Collier nodded. "Yes. We suspected it from the beginning, but we couldn't prove it. It didn't make sense that the victim of a crime would join with her abuser to harm the people who'd stepped in to help her. But the records don't show the whole story. She never testified, so it wasn't clear how she felt. Mariah's part in it all was a blank spot until we spoke to you and Bobbie."

"You bugged my house."

She nodded, but looked at me directly, not breaking eye contact. "You're a smart woman, you had to have suspected this. Maybe not even consciously, but it's hard for me to imagine you didn't know."

I nodded. Probably a part of me did know. Or maybe my baby-brain had rendered me particularly vulnerable to manipulation. Either way, I felt stupid.

"So we can go home?"

"You can, but I wouldn't suggest going home until you call one of these businesses." She pushed forward the brochures and business cards.

"Is there something left to...clean?

Collier nodded. "That's not part of what we do. And the way she...the way it happened, bombings aren't easy to clean up. They take some professional help."

A flash of the moment of explosion, my mind filling in all the blanks: her chest exploding outward, her face obscured by the debris. I didn't see it, but I'd imagined it over and over again. Once, I had accidentally watched footage of a man wearing a home-made explosive collar. He was unable to get out of it. He sat on the ground, in shock, surrounded by police officers who didn't know what to do or how to help him. He screamed something inaudible and then his head and face were no longer visible, no longer there — smoke and pieces of flying metal obscured whatever happened to his head, but his body fell back. Maybe that was how it had been with Mariah, too.

I shook my head to get the image out, the sound of that man's shriek before the explosion.

"Thanks," I told her. "And thanks for letting me know."

I looked down at the brochures. Places that specialized in cleaning up organic material. Organic material. That's what was left of Mariah now. The organic material of the ashes split between me and Bobbie and the organic material left on my lawn. I had placed her ashes in the closet, in the same box I'd been handed at the funeral home. The people at the funeral home had been kind and soothing. Four older men, all brothers, wearing neat suits, slim cut, in variations of gray and blue. Funeral homes and crematoriums tend to be a family business, they explained, when I idly asked them what made them go into the funeral business. I had not really wanted to know, it was just something to do with my mouth, but they must have gotten used to this idle, anxious talk from the grieving. They told me the business had been handed down for three generations already, and their children intended to continue the tradition. It made sense. It would take a whole family to hold so much grief.

"We'll keep in touch," Collier said, leaving the brochures on the bed.

Do we have to? I almost asked, but instead, I nodded. Stefan hadn't been caught yet, and my connection to him was considered useful. Collier had told me that things weren't quite over yet, but I hoped they were for me, at least.

I called several of the cleaners and set up an appointment with the one who answered the phone in person first. I didn't even register the cost, just said yes to everything. I wanted them to wipe away any trace of what had happened. After the crime scene cleaners finished, I left Faun with Colin and took Watson to drive the winding road up to the house and parked in the driveway, far enough away from the house to see it all from a distance. It looked the same as always. The snow was melting. By now it was March, and while it would be silly to call it Spring weather exactly, you could feel the possibility of Spring in the air. An edge of warmth, the snowfall melting into mud that would plague every entranceway until June, when the land finally settled into warmth, after much coaxing.

The dog scratched at the window and whined to be outside, but I couldn't get out of the car. They had cleaned it up, yes, but there were still traces of what had happened. Two broken kitchen windows, covered over with cardboard and duct tape, some remnants of ash on the front door, gashes in the door and siding where the shards of metal and nails had cut through. If I could see it from a distance, then how much would I be able to see up close?

I could not go back there. I drove away and instead parked at a nearby lookout point that faced a little valley town between the mountains. I played my usual game of trying to find the white spire of the churches, often the tallest structures in these little towns. I opened the passenger door and let out Watson, who wrapped himself around my legs, going in circles, wild to be within the vicinity of home and not locked up in a hotel room. I walked him for an hour, until he was panting and my legs ached. We followed a ridge trail, then back again. I took it slow, pausing to notice the places where grass was poking up through the iced-over weeds from last season. I kept my mind on my feet, on the world around me, until my brain settled, until I could think. Then, back at the car, my red cheeks blazing from the cold that was just beginning to transform into pain, I called Colin and told him I couldn't go back to that house, not now and maybe not ever.

I could feel him wanting to protest. He loved that house. It was our house, the place we'd taken Faun home to when we got back from the hospital, where Watson had been a puppy sliding across the wooden floors. It had been his family home before I ever came on the scene. I understood it meant more to him than the place where my sister died, but I couldn't see a way out of that feeling.

"For how long?"

"I don't know."

I could feel through the phone that he wanted to say more, to convince me, but he didn't try to at the moment. "What do you want to do about our living situation until then?" He simply asked.

"I guess the hotel, still."

"Why don't we rent a place here in town for a while. Just until we figure out a permanent solution?"

I agreed, grateful that he was willing to drop it, to just go along with me for now. We found a nice duplex with a backyard in town, right next to an old-fashioned soda shoppe (with that spelling exactly) and a thrift store connected to a free clinic. I liked walking Faun around the little square, taking her to shop for a free sample cup of cream soda while I tried to read or listen to a podcast while sipping their weak, milky coffee.

Months later, after Faun had started zooming around the

apartment, walking at full speed (she never crawled, just went straight from wobbly steps to a full run the next day), Collier called me.

"We've got Agape. Stefan. We've got him and we're holding him for questioning."

For a while after Mariah died, I couldn't read the many articles and videos and documentaries that came out about The Friendship Circle. Eventually, though, I wanted to understand and thought maybe people outside of the situation could see it more clearly. So I went about it like it was my job, watching everything I could get my hands on, from YouTube videos of women putting on makeup while narrating my sister's death to trashy, true-crime shows where terrible actors in bad wigs re-enacted supposed events. I remember watching in shock as I saw a fictionalized version of me (suitably exhausted-looking, a limp ponytail with strands of hair escaping and a baby on her hip, but somehow both thinner and curvier, her v-neck t-shirt revealing a little shadow of cleavage) and a fictionalized version of Mariah (the actor playing Mariah wore heavy makeup and her hair was long and platinum blonde, as Mariah's had been in her teenage years). The show made our last meeting a confrontation. In the re-enactment, Mariah tore open her jacket and revealed her chest, covered in stray wires and an enormous dial. In the re-enactment, I shouted at her to stop, but she turned around and left the house. Then, the windows crashed inward and the scene ended and a cult expert came on screen, her name and credentials listed below her chest. She wore a blazer and pink lipstick, her lips poorly lined, the lines escaping the bounds of her mouth. She talked about my sister's Stockholm syndrome, her twisted desire to get even with anyone who had gotten between her and Stefan and Willow, even her own sister.

"Stockholm Syndrome is mostly bullshit," I told the TV, but she kept talking anyway.

"There's no definitive proof of it, but based on my profile, I believe Mariah came to that house to kill her own sister along with herself. Something happened that prevented her from being able to follow through with that plan. Maybe Chelsea was able to soften Mariah's heart just enough to save herself and her baby, but not enough to save her sister. We'll never know exactly what happened until Chelsea comes forward with her side of the story."

I wanted to hit this woman with the inexpertly lined lips, overplucked brows, and boxy blazer. I wanted to reach through the screen and stuff my fist into her mouth to make all the speculation stop. I paused, noticing that I'd stopped breathing, that I was holding my fists tight at my sides. I tried to breathe. I turned off the television. This woman was just doing what most people do when something anomalous happens. She was trying to master it by knowing, or pretending to know.

Bobbie and I had been contacted by multiple Hollywood people, from the tackiest true crime shows with sloppy reconstructions and lurid names (*Women who KILL*, *Sisters on the EDGE*) to premium television offering me the chance to have Amy Adams play me in the limited series version of our story. Of course, anyone could make a movie out of anything without our approval, and many would, but my approval and input would be a boon. We'd turned them all down. Not because we were above the idea of money or because we didn't want to tell our side of the story. The trouble was that we didn't know what our side of the story was. I don't think many people understand how disorienting it is to be in the middle of something you do not fully understand and didn't agree to. This was Mariah's story, and only she really knew what had happened, and why, and she had robbed me of the opportunity to ever know. All I could do was clean up the mess after.

June, 2017

As the coverage increased and more details came out about Stefan, Willow, and the upstate New York chapter of The Friendship Circle, Bobbie came to visit me. She was thinner than when I'd last visited and wore her usual outfit of corduroys and pullovers with a revolving array of cardigans. She'd cut her hair short, the usual pixie she'd worn most of my life, but this time I could see her scalp around the temples, and her hair was mostly gray now. She sat at our kitchen table over a cup of tea, just as Mariah had.

"I wanted to ask you about all these shows. All the calls we're getting."

"I've said no to everybody," I told her. "I can't be part of whatever the fuck all of this is, this whole industry of misery farming. I see her face everywhere."

Bobbie nodded. "That's what I mean. It's becoming...it's becoming something I'm ashamed of, to be honest with you."

"You can't help what people say about her."

"No, but we could be part of the conversation. Nobody's getting the real Mariah because we're not telling them about her."

"Do you know who the real Mariah was?" I asked Bobbie. "Because I sure as fuck don't."

"She was our Mariah. She loved nineteenth century literature and she loved you. She was the kindest kid I ever met. Nobody knows that about her. She was a lot of things."

"If she loved me, then why did she come to my house with a bomb on her chest?"

The week I was in bed, thinking over that day, replaying the entire conversation in my head until I could run it back a recording, slowing it down, focusing on her hand on the coffee cup, my head started to clear and I began to get angry with Mariah. I remembered the moment when she had Faun pressed against her jacket, the jacket she wore to cover up the bomb strapped to her chest. She had come to see me only to die in the most dramatic way possible right in my front yard. What if I'd refused to let her go outside alone? Would she have set off that bomb if I'd been standing next to her? What if I'd been holding the baby?

Bobbie shook her head. "I don't believe — "

"She came to my house, specifically, to die. Why would she do that if it wasn't to hurt me, bodily or emotionally or whatever?"

Bobbie took my hand in hers and squeezed it hard.

"Maybe she went to you because she needed one last comfort before she did Stefan's bidding. You think he wanted her to come out of this alive?"

"Mariah said she was part of the plan, that it had been her idea as well as his."

"Honey, what cult leaders make you do is believe that the

work you do at their bidding is all your own idea. That's pretty much the MO."

Of course, The Friendship Circle had been a cult. That's what every documentary said. Former members had recently stepped forward and discussed "the ways that a seemingly benign group had become an authoritarian nightmare," according to the voiceover for one of the documentaries. The three most high-profile members were Stefan, obviously, but also Mariah and the other bomber, a young man named Oliver. Oliver had also killed himself after coming home to his parents to say goodbye, though in a completely different way. He had hanged himself in his childhood closet after telling his elderly parents he was going up to take a nap, he'd be down again soon for dinner. This left only Stefan, the assumed mastermind of the bombings.

"Do you think it's true that he made them do these things? How is that possible to do with adults?"

Bobbie clicked her tongue at me as though I'd said something ridiculous. "He's had his hooks in her since she was fifteen years old. She has built her whole life around what happened then, her whole sense of self since then. She was his perfect victim. Of course he was responsible, in one way or another."

"Is that what you want people to understand? That she didn't have a chance?" I didn't like this idea, either, that Mariah was just some doll he played with for the last fifteen years of her life, none of her choices truly her own. She hadn't just made a beeline to self destruction. She'd gone to Vienna to study graduate work to be a therapist. She'd been a seeker. How could she have done all of these things with her life while being asleep to some bomb Stefan and Willow had set inside her?

Bobbie shrugged. "Maybe she did have a chance. God knows she made some choices herself. But I also know she wasn't the same child after it happened. That has to mean something."

It has to mean something. It's strange that we believe things like this, that something must have meaning, even if it doesn't appear to, on the surface, as though meaning were a thing that exists inherently and not a construction made from the raw material of memory.

"If you think we should talk, we'll talk." I said. "But I want us to be in control of it as much as possible and to agree on the message."

Bobbie nodded. "I'd never go forward with any of this unless you agreed to it." She reached out her hands to clasp mine, which was nervously twirling a teabag string around my index finger. I read the inspirational message on the tag: *open yourself to life and it will open up for you.* I laughed, then met her eyes.

"Hey," she said. "You still here in the room with me?"

I nodded.

"There was more to her than her death. More to her than Stefan and Willow. That's all true. And also, they did alter her. She was affected by them. That's true, too. Both things can be true."

Bobbie had changed in the last fifteen years. She was softer, less solid but in a way that suited her — that core Bobbie was there, but it was easier to access, her warmth freer. I reached out and squeezed her hand.

"You're right. I guess I'm just looking for evidence that

she was still herself. You didn't see her, Bobbie. She was skin and bones. I thought I had her, the real Mariah. She was seeming like her old self, she was really talking to me. And then, she walked away and did this."

There it was, the sticky part. I'd thought I could trust her, that she was really and truly with me, that she was going to turn herself in. I flashed back to Willow in her living room on that day when I received the phone call from mom. I had trusted her, too. She had appeared to truly care for me, to really want to comfort me. And maybe she had. And Maybe Mariah had truly been with me, for those moments, before some other, unknowable part of her fired up and took the reins.

Most people, thank God, will never know the strangeness of mourning a public person, a person known only for the terrible thing they did at the end of their life and nothing that came before it. People knew the information, that my mother was an alcoholic, that Mariah had lived in Vienna, they knew the broad strokes of what had happened to her that summer, but they didn't know her. I had been watching those shows for a taste of what it had been like to know her, hoping that maybe somebody could capture it, but nobody did. Most likely, you can't capture anything about the quality of a person in a movie. Maybe everybody who loved somebody who dies dramatically looks at the footage about them, looking for something to hold onto. Here I was, looking to strangers for clues about my sister, whom I'd held as a baby, rubbing her soft head against my cheek as we both would drift off into sleep, who died in such a violent, spectacular way that it almost erased everything else I thought I'd know about her.

September, 2017

Not long after she notified me about Stefan's capture, Collier called to tell me they were starting to build the case against him.

"Thank you for telling me," I said, surprised they would waste precious time notifying me. I hadn't heard from either agent in months and liked it that way.

Collier cleared her throat. "I called for more than just a courtesy. We've got him for now, but we need your help to keep him."

"What do you need from me?"

"He won't talk without seeing you first. He named you specifically and said before he told us anything, he wanted to talk to you. He said he needed to 'get a few things off his chest.'"

"I don't want to talk to him."

I could imagine the things he'd have to say. If he wanted to kill the people who fostered his kids, imagine what he wanted to do to me. As much as I hated him, I didn't have any desire to confront him. What would be the point? It would only give him an opportunity to hurt me.

"I know how hard this is for you," she said. "And we all know this man is a master manipulator. It wasn't just Mariah and Oliver he had making bombs — who do you think assembled them and did the research to find where to send them? He had a whole collection of helpers who never fully understood why they were doing what they were doing, just that he'd given the orders and they had to comply. This is why it's so important he tells us everything, and why we need you."

I bit my lip, hard, to calm myself, and took a deep breath before speaking. "Isn't there enough to convict him already?"

"It looks that way to you, but it's not so easy. He's going to be put on trial, and when he's on trial, he's going to say the things that every cult leader says: these people made their own choices and I didn't coerce them. These were educated, well-read adults who made up their own minds. Some of those choices were bad ones, but that wasn't his fault. And in this case, it could absolutely look true from the outside. He didn't drug them or sexually assault them or physically abuse them, not in ways people recognize as such — though we are working on that angle. If we don't get to the heart of why these people followed him, we might be missing something very big. Many cults start out with one figurehead but end up branching off into hundreds. You never know which one is going to be a problem and which is simply a bunch of people living their lives as they choose."

"He's not going to tell me anything of use to you. He hates me. And I doubt, even if I talk to him, that he'll tell you anything more than he intended to anyway."

"That's why you're the perfect person to handle this.

Anger might trip him up, or better yet, you might rattle him into telling the truth. According to our profiling, Stefan is a classic narcissist: he'll talk if you give him an audience, and you'll be the perfect audience. He'll want to hurt you, yes, but his desire to hurt you will override his self-preservation. As of right now, he's claiming that every criminal act was due to the choices of other individuals. He sent a lot of packages himself, he tells us, often filled with things nobody told him about, because he was simply being a servant." She said the word with distaste and I realized she disliked him personally, not just as a murderer-by-proxy. We were aligned in that, at least.

"Will you help us?"

I'd never visited a prison before, but the detectives prepared me as well as they could. I had to remove my jewelry and leave it in a locker, taking a plastic key fob with me to claim it again later. The key fob was rubbery, no hard edges or the possibility that I could make it into a weapon. They patted me down and led me to a small room where I was separated from another small room by filmy, scratched plastic, not the smooth, clean glass of the movies. Somebody had carved a big, loopy heart into the plastic, right where I could see a dim reflection of my own face. A telephone hung on the wall to my right, the neutral, beige receiver browned mid-handle, where thousands of hands had previously gripped it.

When the doors opened, Stefan emerged. I recognized him immediately, though he was an old man now. His hair was still long and black, though now his face was covered with a salt and pepper beard, mostly salt. When he sat down and bent over to scoot his chair up to the desk, I saw the gray roots at his scalp, two inches growing in a completely even line. He'd dyed his hair. I remembered that summer, how he had his shirts all unbuttoned to reveal his chest, his long hair and cologne, always a rich, strange scent, not something you'd get from a department store but some concoction of essential oils. He'd always been vain, always cultivated a particular look, smell, a complete atmosphere to envelop you in. He was meant to intoxicate a particular kind of person, to fulfill specific longings. I could see the careful cultivation now that he was mostly stripped of it.

He sat down and looked up, giving me a long, evaluative look. He smiled.

I picked up the telephone, and he did, too. I wore an earpiece where Collier could give me suggestions or prompt me if needed, which I hoped he couldn't see, so I pulled my hair down over my ears. I'd initially dressed up for the meeting, then taken off most of the makeup and changed into what I now considered my "leaving the house" clothes — not sweatpants, but in the same family, clothes I could throw a cardigan over but also comfortably wear to bed. I looked normal, fine. He wouldn't think I'd dressed up for him, but he also wouldn't think that I'd spent the day anxious and depressed, my eyes red, clothes rumpled. I wanted to present a neutral canvas. Better for him to project whatever he wanted onto it.

"Chelsea," he said. I couldn't register an emotion on his face, but he looked me in the eye. "I was so sorry to hear about Mariah."

"Fuck you," I said, before I'd even considered a response. Whoops.

"Take a breath," Collier advised me over the earpiece. "Get your heart rate down." I breathed in deeply and slowly, careful not to let him see my gasping for breath, but didn't take my eyes off of him.

"I can imagine it feels good to say that to me," Stefan said.

"Damn right it does."

"There's the old Chelsea I remember, flinging her anger and her fear at everyone else, hoping to avoid responsibility for her part in her own pain. That's how Mariah described you, right before she left. Bitter and old were the exact words, if I remember correctly." His jaw twitched, but his tense, slightly mocking expression landed at last into an ugly, tight smile.

So it was starting right away. What had seemed at first like blankness was instead bottled-up fury. His jaw and mouth were tight, his eyebrows drawn together. His mouth moved in between his words, as though it was beyond his control. He hated me. I looked at this old man, hair dye growing out, thin and frail-looking where I could see his wrists coming out of the cuffs, his orange jumpsuit baggy on his body. And I hated him, too, no matter how weak he looked, how powerless he now was.

"They said you wanted to talk to me and I'm here," I said, avoiding his gaze to pick a piece of imaginary lint from my sleeve.

"Good job," Collier said into my earpiece. "The more solid you are, the more unbalanced he's going to be. He's looking for a reaction. Remember that. Keep your seat."

He nodded. "I just wanted to see if you understand now

what it's like to have everything taken from you."

I steadied myself by looking down at the table, where people had, somehow, carved their names into the wood with whatever sharp materials they'd managed to smuggle into the room. Maybe they'd used their fingernails in desperation to make their feelings and protestations and statements of devotion more permanent. Some had made drawings of hearts with the names of their lovers inside, maybe the same people who had scratched that heart into the plastic, the heart now filled with Stefan's face. Somebody here had loved the person on the other side of the barrier. They had imagined themselves together, willing it to be so by putting their names together in a semi-permanent state on this institutional plastic.

He was wrong. I didn't understand what it was like to have everything taken from me because I still had so much, despite losing Mariah. I hadn't really thought of it that way before, that I still have so much. I have built a life, a life that I for the most part love.

Fuck, I thought. He didn't destroy me. He didn't get in my head. And then, I knew what to say.

"Were you surprised to hear I was still alive? Was I part of the plan?"

He kept himself very still. He, too, was thinking.

"It was a big explosion, from what I heard," he said. "I can't say I didn't hope Mariah could at least take you along with her, if she was going to choose to go out like that."

"Choose," I repeated.

He smiled, back on solid ground. "Everybody chooses,

Chelsea. Even not making a choice is a choice. You can't get away from choices."

"I'm not one of your followers," I said. "I'm not looking for your wisdom. I just want to know why you've asked me here."

He nodded. "I wanted to talk to you about that. Not to you, but to the people listening in." He tapped the phone at his ear, a knock resounding painfully in my own. "The idea that I've got followers or that Mariah or anyone else was doing what I told them to do, that's a real twisted take on things. You knew your sister well: wasn't she the most free spirit you can imagine? Could anyone make her do anything she didn't want to do?"

"You don't get to tell me who Mariah was."

"Oh, I think I knew her better than you ever did. After all, she was done with you. Had been for a long time."

He was baiting me with an idea I'd had turning in my head for years. He couldn't hurt me with something I'd already hurt myself with. For once, my self-loathing was serving me well.

"I still don't understand why I'm here. You could have told them all that yourself. Seems like you aren't done with me. Seems like I'm living rent free in your head, as the kids say."

I cracked a smile at my own joke. He didn't.

"You're here because I wanted you to be here, so we'll talk about what I want to talk about." He said. "They want you here to get information, but what I care about is the truth. So I'll tell you the truth."

He smiled a big, expansive smile, and I flashed back to one of those dinners, when he'd sat close to me, showering me with attention and praise. I remembered his body, how he would put himself slightly closer to me than he should have, pushing himself up against my shoulder, keeping me close to him physically. It was intoxicating to be close to somebody who seemed so beautifully himself, who seemed to like me, too. I was just a kid, trying to be an adult, and here was a person who seemed so unapologetic, so solid and clear about who he was, what he wanted. I remembered how casually Willow and Stefan would reach out and pull me close, as if there were no boundaries between us. At the time, the touch had seemed both comforting and strange, wrong in a way I didn't know how to articulate. I had felt ashamed for wanting to pull away, so I'd allowed it, and then I felt shame for allowing it, shame when it did feel good and I wanted more.

We had been so young, our need had been so close to the surface. I remembered what Mariah had said before the explosion, about Willow: Sometimes I wondered why she didn't stop it, slow it down, why it wasn't good enough for me to be her child, and her to be like my mom.

"The truth is that this is the outcome of what you set in motion all those years ago. You did this," Stefan said.

Maybe five years ago I would have accepted this, swallowed his words whole, but I couldn't: I didn't believe it anymore. He thought I really was the person Mariah told him I was, full of guilt and shame and misery, unhappy with my life and desperate to make up for whatever error she thought I'd made.

I couldn't help myself: I rolled my eyes. "You're a rapist and you got caught. That seems like the only relevant truth here. Sounds like this is what you've set in motion, and now you're in prison and I'm free."

Stefan sat back in his seat, keeping the grin on his face, though his mouth twitched.

"Everything I've ever done has been with consent," Stefan said. "You know a lot of these *laws* are bullshit." He swept his hand as though swatting a fly at the word laws. "You know well that young women have sexual needs too, that they can consent. To say otherwise is pretty ridiculous. I know you remember, Chelsea, how you'd slide up close to me, practically begging to be touched."

I don't know what kind of reaction he was looking for, but I shuddered. I hoped he didn't see the reaction — I suspected any reaction was enough. Repulsion, attraction, anything revealed would mean something had hit. So I bit the inside of my mouth. He saw something anyway. "I think you wanted to be close to me but didn't know how. Wouldn't allow yourself."

He watched me carefully, seeing the ways his words affected me. He watched my face for subtle changes, as he had when I was a teenager. I remembered this, what I'd seen as attentiveness and care at the time. It wasn't that at all. He was watching for an opening.

"You were afraid. Mariah was never afraid, but you were. That day when you posed for the painting, I remember how eagerly you undressed, how you shifted underneath the fabric. You liked it, you liked being looked at, being admired. And then, by the end, you'd gone blank, afraid of your own desire. Your eyes by the end were dark and empty. And I see it right now, how dark you are beneath whatever this is, whatever face you're wearing now to hide all that fear."

"Maybe I was afraid because I understood you. I knew who you really were. You tried to fool me, to make me feel safe, but you were never safe."

He laughed. "Who am I, really?"

I shrugged. "Just a disgusting pervert."

He laughed again, this time with what sounded like genuine mirth. I felt a pang of fear: I'd miscalculated. I could feel him coiling up from behind the glass.

He shook his head. "You're full of hangups, even now. You can't imagine life beyond your husband and your kid and your dog."

That verified it, Mariah had told him about my life, or at least her version of how she imagined it looked. I could guess how she described it — small and provincial with nothing anchoring me to some larger sense of purpose. But it hadn't felt like that when she visited. I'd sensed nothing cruel or mocking in her in that hour we spent together. But then again, she probably needed me to have failed, to be unhappy and trapped so she wouldn't have to look at herself. I understood that. It even gave me a feeling of tenderness toward her. She could tell Stefan terrible things about me and still care for me. I held on to the Mariah who could be everything at once. I put any anger or shame or fear in a box that I'd open later. No time for it now. Now, I had to destroy him somehow.

Stefan spoke. "I remember that night you came to dinner at our house after you'd slept with that guy, what was his name? I can't remember. That guy with a girlfriend. Your eyes were red. You were distraught, that's what Mariah told us, you were distraught and you needed us to help you feel better."

I didn't answer this. I watched his face, his body, and, like him, scanned for signs of vulnerability.

He nodded as though I'd answered. "You came to the house because you knew we would care for you. You used us, and when it was no longer useful, you got rid of us."

I laughed, I couldn't help it. He could only understand relationships as transactional. No wonder he thought the worst of me.

This made him drop his smile for a moment, the skin on his face sagging like a mask sliding right off the bones.

"Funny you kept on seeing him even after he was engaged."

It was my turn to drop my smile.

He nodded again. "And that professor, how long did that go on? Those phone calls he'd take from his wife right after he fucked you, how you could hear the baby crying in the background."

I felt this one in my stomach. I didn't remember telling Mariah these things, but I imagine I had on some desperate night when I wanted to tell somebody about all the memories that burdened me. I had probably told her drunk during one of the rare times she called me in those early years of our estrangement, when I had hope each time that I could get her back on my side if I was just honest enough.

"You wonder how I know all of this about you."

It took all the effort I had to simply shrug.

He went on as though I had answered. "Mariah told me most of it, but I could also guess what happened to you. Sleeping with older, unavailable men because you didn't feel confident enough to find somebody who would love you for yourself. And look at you now. I can see how fat you've gotten, how clumsy your makeup is. I see you've become a middle-aged woman before your time — you aren't even thirty-seven yet, are you? Looks like you settled, finally. Had that baby before you dried up. Married some boring man you aren't even sure you love."

I wasn't stunned by his insight. I wasn't even upset. He was going about this all wrong. I was ashamed about the past, not about now. I was a middle aged woman with a pooch of fat that ruined every outfit that involved a tucked-in shirt. My makeup was casual, my hair full of split ends since I hadn't gotten it cut since the baby was born. And I didn't regret any of it.

"Don't respond," Collier said in my ear. "Smile, shrug, do something that shows him he isn't in your head."

"Did you bring me here to reminisce?" I asked, feigning casualness.

"I just want you to know that I understand you. You're weak, and weak people are dangerous."

"Have you ever heard of projection?" I asked. "The only person here who's ever hurt anyone is you. Maybe you're the weak one." This felt too easy.

He didn't like the answer, but he simply shrugged.

"I didn't directly hurt anyone."

I smiled. "Neither did Charles Manson."

He laughed. "Maybe he was innocent, then."

I shrugged. "Makes sense you'd say that."

We looked at each other. I didn't look away, and the longer I didn't look away, the more his face hardened, his mouth went thin and tight.

"Why do you really want me here?" I asked, the moment I sensed he might be readying to speak. "I love catching up, but I've got a kid to take care of."

"I need you to know what you took from me." He said. The word *kid* had clouded his face. I'd hit on something real.

"So tell me."

"Willow. She had cancer. We didn't find out it had come back until she got out of prison. She came out sick, her body wrecked."

It was astonishing to see something human pass across his face, the pain of her death.

"I got out in time to watch her die slowly. If she'd been out, maybe she never would have gotten cancer. Or maybe she would have, but we'd have caught it early. You might as well have killed her."

"My children won't see me," he continued. "They're all adults now, even the youngest. I've never met their children and never will. They went through hell in those years without us. Persephone went to rehab. River had a drinking problem. If I'd been there, this never would have happened. You did this to them."

His accusations flew off of me as though I was wearing some protective coating. I had enough time to register this thrilling lack of pain. I didn't believe a word he was saying. I hadn't caused the pain these children had gone through. I remember the children on that day, I could see their fear and confusion and pain, but it wasn't mine.

Collier said something in my ear, but I didn't hear it. I was watching him closely, thinking of how to respond.

"If anyone's responsible for all the shit that happened, it's you," I said.

He continued without responding, as he had throughout the conversation. He wasn't really listening to me, I could tell — he was listening for tone, for information he could pluck out and use. I didn't need to waste time responding carefully to him, I just had to respond with something that lit the right circuits.

"Mariah sought me out, did you know that?" He continued. "She wrote to us as soon as she was able to, when she turned eighteen. When I got out, Mariah was there waiting for me. She was there in the room with Willow when she died. And she was there when I decided I needed to find a new way to live, that I had a message for people who, like me, felt that the state had wronged them. She came with me, willingly, and we joined The Family Circle."

"I can believe that," I said. "She's always been loyal. What I can't believe is that she'd agree to the bombings unless she felt she had to."

"She wanted to do something to right the wrong that happened. It was a kind of protest. I couldn't stop her from doing what she pleased."

"By sending a bomb to a sixty-year-old former foster parent? Killing a social worker?"

"They were all part of a system. Mariah understood the system itself was rotten."

I shook my head. "Sure it is. But not the way you're saying.

You told her who the enemy was and expected her to follow you."

"She saw the injustice with her own eyes. I didn't have to convince her who the enemy was."

This was getting me nowhere. He smiled, enjoying watching me squirm. I couldn't argue with him. It gave him energy.

I waited for some guidance from Collier, keeping eye contact.

"Get personal." Collier said in my ear. "Question his authority. He wants you to know he's in charge while never saying enough for us to pin it on him. I need you to make him feel small, then he'll have to say it."

Stefan laughed, watching me listen. I saw his eyes go bright and amused, suddenly understanding.

"You waiting for your orders?"

It didn't matter if he knew. Hell, maybe it even helped — he could feel superior for a minute. A bigger audience, isn't that what every narcissist wants? I could give him that. "So if you didn't ask her to do it, then what? She was the architect of the whole thing?"

Stefan shrugged. "I don't know — I was merely a servant among servants."

"Funny you were so out of the loop you didn't even know what she was up to."

He paused. "I knew she wanted to help right the wrongs that were done to us. She wanted to make an example."

"And you let her do that."

Stefan held out his hands in supplication. "Who am I to stop anyone from doing something they feel called to do?"

"But you cared about her, or so you say. You knew it wouldn't end well for her, but you let it happen anyway."

He leaned forward, crowding the space between us. I wanted to lean back, but I did the opposite: I leaned forward, too. He was behind plastic, one hand cuffed to the table. Any gesture he made to intimidate me was illogical, ridiculous, even. If I could remember that, then I could get to him.

"She loved me. I loved her," he said. "Sometimes when you love people you take risks."

"It seems like she was more willing to take risks than you. I thought if you loved somebody you protected them, you don't put them at risk and save your own ass."

"Good," Collier said in my ear. "Keep going."

Stefan grimaced. "I don't think love has the same kinds of limits that you do, Chelsea. Your world is small and full of rules."

"I remember that night you had me come over to paint me differently from how you remember it. I remember feeling sick, but going along with it anyway because I trusted you both. No, scratch that. I trusted Willow. I could feel something off about you."

Stefan shrugged. "And did anything bad happen to you, Chelsea? I didn't touch you. You walked away from that room whole and happy."

I felt the words come out without calculation. "But Mariah didn't."

"Mariah never did anything she didn't want to do. I've told

you that. You know it in your heart."

There it was, that gleaming opening I was looking for.

"I thought so, but when I saw her that day, she looked beaten down, Stefan. She looked…not like herself. Like a zombie. I don't think she was choosing anything at all."

He laughed. "If she wasn't choosing anything herself, then why are you alive?"

I feigned shock, letting my mouth hang open, shaking my head slowly as though I couldn't process what he was saying. I could see him take in my face, could see his delight.

"What do you mean?" I asked.

"What I mean is that if she couldn't think for herself, then why are you alive?"

"I don't understand."

"No," he said, jerking his hand against the handcuff. "You wouldn't understand, would you? Mariah was devoted. When it was all over, when they were closing in on us, as we knew they would eventually, she performed her last act of love for me and went to your house. She told me she was going to detonate inside the house, with your dog and your child and your husband, the only three creatures in the world who give a fuck about you. Maybe it was a moment of fear — you carry it like a disease around with you — or a moment of mercy that made her step outside instead of following the plan. But it was her choice, the last one she ever made."

Stefan sat back, pleased with the look on my face, whatever it was. I had not been able to hold my acting. The longer he spoke, the more flashes of that day came through,

I pressed my fingernails against my palm until I felt the pain and looked up at him, meeting his eyes.

"When we last spoke, she expressed nothing but excitement at being rid of you," Stefan said.

In my ear, Collier said "We've got enough, okay? He knew about the bombings. He didn't stop them. It's enough." Maybe she could sense I wasn't present anymore. I had checked out and could see myself from a distance, my shoulders slumped. She didn't want me to fuck it up by getting emotional. But I didn't care about her investigation anymore. I felt my feet on the ground. I breathed in. I wasn't in the house anymore. Mariah had died and that was all true, but it was over.

I remembered that summer, the children at the dinner table, the joy as well as the manipulation, because some of the joy had been real. Just being in that room with a family that felt complete, that felt whole in a way I'd never felt before. Then, I remembered the day they took the children away, the doll on the ground, Persephone reaching back to her mother. He'd had what we had wanted so badly and he couldn't manage to keep it. Somehow, it wasn't enough for him.

"What a waste," I said simply. I felt deflated, all of the anger and rage had flown out of me and all I had left was exhausted sadness. On that last day, Mariah had chosen me. She could have chosen him, but she didn't. I had been loved, even if imperfectly. And here was this pathetic man, still trying to feel important, still needing something from me.

"You had a beautiful family," I said. "I would have given everything to grow up and be like you both, to have a big art grant and these brilliant, funny, talented kids in a big, beautiful house. It must have been a horror to realize you destroyed it all because other people just aren't real to you."

I spoke slowly, and he didn't try to respond or interrupt. Something was happening between us that wasn't about the detective in my ear. Collier started to speak again, but I needed to focus, I needed to keep my seat, so I removed the earpiece, letting him see me place it on the table before me. He looked down, then back up at me.

"How terrible it must have been to throw all that away. I bet you feel so much regret. Maybe you had to do something big, to make it feel like you were not the one responsible for your own life falling apart. But you were. It was always you. You must feel so much shame and embarrassment that everyone sees you as you are now. Grey hair, wrinkles, your body getting soft and saggy."

Stefan and I met eyes.

"No matter what I did, at least my kids are still alive. You abandoned Mariah."

"I let her choose the life she wanted, and she turned to you. That's what killed her. You."

Stefan and I kept our eyes on each other. I wanted to turn away from him, to break that gaze, but I refused to be the first one.

"She did turn to me. She turned to me and I put trust in her, but you know what? She was weak. She was like you. I wanted you to die with her. But she was weak, and couldn't even fucking do that for me, after every misery she caused me, after everything you took away from me."

Stefan leaned forward and spoke slowly, quietly.

"You had better pray that I'm here for life. If I'm ever out, you'll find no peace. I will find you myself and wring your neck with my own hands, just to make sure you're dead. I'll find your child and what I do to her will make what happened to Mariah look like a walk in the park. I'll kill your fucking dog, Chelsea. You will have nothing. So you better wish that I never get my freedom again."

I smiled, with great effort, the waves of fear and sickness rising up in me.

"Oh, I think you've pretty much granted my wish all by yourself because you can't keep your fucking mouth shut." With that, I snatched up the earpiece and jogged out, reaching the trash can by the door just in time to throw up what little food I'd managed to eat that morning.

August, 2018

It's notoriously difficult to prosecute cult leaders. They have a power that comes from the vulnerabilities of others. They know who to manipulate into action and who to keep at the edges of plans. They can smell trauma and use that desperate, fearful need for security to create loyalty. This is what the prosecutor said, making her case to the jury.

She called experts to the stand, including a psychologist who specialized in cult deprogramming and trauma bonding. She called an expert in sexual assault who discussed the ways that abusers groom their victims, making them believe that sexual contact creates a bond between them that cannot be broken and a line of demarcation between themselves and the rest of the world. She discussed Mariah's age at the initial contact, fifteen, and the vulnerability of that age, that balance between having a young mind but a desire to enter adulthood, how her being a teenage girl without a father and an alcoholic mother made her far more statistically likely to be vulnerable to a predator, how her loneliness that summer increased the likelihood even more. So much abstract evidence, and still, I couldn't see Mariah, or myself in it.

My meeting with Stefan gave some choice quotes for the prosecution. He all but admitted that he'd wanted me dead, that he faulted Mariah for not being able to follow through with the plan. Far more damning, though, was the evidence from former members who reported that he'd raved about the state, about the individuals who'd later been targeted. Their names had to be memorized, and then later, their addresses. In order to keep the members of his group tired, keep them stupid, they were often deprived of food, of connection to anyone but him. He hadn't physically abused them, but he'd forced their bodies into a state where their rational minds simply weren't functioning anymore. One follower, as pale and thin as Mariah had been, described how she'd spent a week locked in a dark room, given only water and oatmeal to eat, because she had told him that she had doubts about his plans.

"It's not as though he made me go in there," she said. "He didn't use force. He suggested it. He suggested that maybe I needed to spend some time to myself, cut everything down to the basics, get away from the noise. So I went into the room and I ate almost nothing and I drank almost nothing. I did it because I believed I was choosing it. I did it because he told me I was losing faith in the mission and I knew if I lost faith in the mission that I'd have nothing left."

Stefan was found guilty of murder and a cascade of other charges. Coupled with his established history of sexual abuse of minors, he would be spending the rest of his life in prison with no hope of parole. Multiple former cult members and targets of the attacks stood up to speak to him at the trial, testifying to the impact of his crimes. I didn't testify — the statements from my conversation with Stefan were enough. I had watched some footage from the televised trial early on and saw how the cameras would pan to me in response to testimony. I looked pale and severe and miserable the entire time, on the edge of sickness. I showed up every day. I felt I owed it to Mariah to see it to the end. When they sentenced him, he didn't cry, he didn't break down, he simply nodded, glanced back at the audience, trying to find me, to meet my eye. I was in the back, though, by myself. Bobbie had not come — she had arthritis and was recovering from pneumonia, which had knocked her out for two months, so I'd vetoed the trip, saying that I would stay for the both of us. I don't think he identified me in the sea of faces.

When all of this started, Faun was just walking, and when it ended, she could communicate to me in short, clear statements. She had favorite things, like the color green or the texture of my satin robe. She wanted to hold my phone and take photographs herself instead of always being the one photographed. She was able to ride a small car with pedals around the yard. I remember Mariah at this age, endlessly curious, loving to a fault. But the more I tried to remember who Mariah was, what the quality of being with her was like, the more I remembered her sharper edges, memories that I'd smoothed over to give me the Mariah that I wanted, not the Mariah that I'd truly had. The real Mariah was much more interesting than the flighty, angelic, amorphous person I'd created in my mind or in the story I told to the detectives.

Sometimes, she'd get so angry she'd throw things, like once when I beat her at horseshoes and she threw the horseshoe directly at me, banging me in the upper arm and creating a huge, purple bruise that inspired the school nurse to call me out of class and ask if I was being abused at home. I remembered how, afterward, she came to me, crying, saying that she was sorry, that she'd just gotten so mad. She hadn't succumbed to Stefan because she was weak as he had said. She was stubborn and kind and sweet and loving and loyal. The loyalty is the part that stands after me now, since I got the letter.

After the trial, Collier showed up at our front door. By now, Watson knew her and greeted her with excitement, leaning his body against her knees to get her attention. She grimaced at her now fur-covered black slacks but patted him gamely until he bounded away back to the living room, looking for a toy to find and present to her.

She held a manila folder in her hands with my name on it. Mariah's handwriting.

"We had to wait until after the trial to give you this."

I motioned her over to the couch, but she shook her head and nodded toward the door.

"I have to make this quick — I'm on my way down to the city." She held out the envelope again.

I didn't take it immediately. "How am I going to feel after I read this?"

She shrugged. "I am going to tell you the truth: if I felt this was going to destroy you, you'd never see it. I don't even have to give it to you. But I am, because I think it will help you."

"Help me what?"

"Help you understand exactly where her mind was when she came to your house. I know it bothers you, that she put you in danger. Maybe this will help."

I nodded and took the envelope.

Dear Chelsea,

I hope you'll get to read this note. I intend for you to get it, but I don't know what might happen. Maybe I'm just writing to myself and this note will just end up in some pile of evidence. Maybe you'll be dead. I'll almost certainly be dead, if all goes well. That's a funny thing to say.

I know for a long time you've wanted to know if I hate you, if I could ever forgive you, all of that, but the truth is I couldn't forgive you. I stayed away because that anger was so deep and so sharp that when I was with you, all I wanted was to hurt you. I don't like feeling that way about you, so I stayed away so I could hold on to some love for you. And I have.

This is also true: you were right. When I was fifteen, I wasn't ready for what happened. Stefan and Willow were so kind and so loving. I didn't want to lose them. I'd do whatever they asked, and did. The more I did, the more I was separate from you. That night you told me about what happened with you and that guy at work, I almost wanted to tell you everything that was happening with Willow and Stefan. I thought maybe because you'd made a mistake, I could tell you about mine. But you fell asleep, and I went back over to their house, and they asked me to invite you over, to invite you to be painted, to be part of the family. They even said it, Chelsea, they said "part of the family," and then I knew I wasn't going to tell you because I wasn't making a mistake. I was adding you to the family, and I had to give you the chance to join. I figured that the bad feeling I had sometimes was just because I was separated from you.

But everything happened so fast after that. I got closer to them. Everything they asked me to do started to feel normal, feel familiar. Going back to you and Bobbie felt lonely, like a place I didn't belong anymore. When something Willow or Stefan wanted to do felt wrong, I'd just stop feeling it, I'd fly off somewhere else in my head.

I did hate you when you told the police. I was embarrassed and angry that your first urge was to tell everyone instead of talk to me. I saw my whole life destroyed, my new family, these people who loved me and promised that after mom died or if she didn't clean up, I could just come live with them. I would fantasize about being one of their kids, but also like another mom to the kids. I was a kid and I thought like a kid. Bobbie said that once when it all happened, that I was just a kid and I'd understand someday. I guess that day has finally arrived, but it's too late.

I've spent a long time by myself here. I had a lot of time to think. I have tried hard to find a way to believe that Stefan and Willow cared about me, that we were meant to be together. I meditated and I studied the shadow and I went to a guru who told me that we are all really ancient bodies so really, there is no age, age is an illusion. I could believe all that. Most days I do. But sometimes, I think back to how it felt that first time, how sick I felt, and I can't find a way to understand it.

I wish you would have come for me and dragged me away. I wish you'd gotten on a plane and flown to wherever I was and forced me to leave with you. I know you couldn't have done that, though, because I never would have let you, and I can't hold it against you.

I am supposed to pull you in next to my chest when I detonate. That's what I told him I'd do. You are the last one on the list, the most important one. We all say your name. People who have never met you know your name and say it like a prayer, only backwards, a name that's meant to light us up with anger. They know this monster version of you that Stefan told them about. I wonder sometimes, though, if I'm really the one he wants gone. Think about it: if he'd never met me, then it never would have happened. I owe it to him to make things better, but I can't do this last thing for him. I'm going to let him down.

Sometimes I look at myself as though at a distance and wonder what I'm going to do next, it's all so confusing anymore. Oliver said I'm not eating enough and that maybe I'm confused because my brain's not getting any food. I pulled out a clump of my own hair in the shower yesterday. I haven't had a period in so long I can't remember the last time I bought a tampon.

I guess what I want to say to you is that I'm worried you were right but there's nothing I can do about it now. I think he senses my lack of devotion to him and the cause. I feel so many things at the same time lately, and my mind is so foggy. I have tried to meditate and I have tried to sit in the darkness and understand but everything comes out confused. All I know is that I feel steady when he's with me and when he tells me why it makes sense. He tells me I need to hold into myself when I'm with you because you can affect me so badly. That has been true in the past. But I want to see you. I hope you let me hold the baby.

I also hope you take the baby far away from me and don't let me touch her.

I'm glad it's going to be over soon. I hope you make it out and I hope whatever happens, if you are reading this, that you can forgive me.

Love,
Mariah

I read the letter in Mariah's voice. I could almost see her sitting at a spare table in the cabin, writing the note painstakingly, her handwriting small and precise. The note was incoherent in places, unclear, both sad and infuriating, but Collier was right — it did help. I could imagine her sitting there, her mind sluggish from starvation, unmoored from the rest of the world for god knows how long, so completely enmeshed with him that it was hard to see beyond it.

I imagine I should have been shocked by the revelation that she was supposed to take me with her, but I wasn't. She hadn't done it — she hadn't even really considered it. The fact that Stefan wanted her to do it, and that even his will couldn't make her hurt me, both angered and soothed me. She hadn't allowed him to take everything from her.

I folded the letter back up and put it in the envelope and then made my way to the attic. I got a rickety step-stool and pulled down the attic door and climbed up the stairs to a room I'd only visited to deposit some boxes of Christmas lights and baby clothes Faun had grown out of. To my great relief, the bare, hanging bulb turned on, and looked around. I couldn't even fully stand up in the room, though I could crawl to where Colin had stacked a few boxes. I found the box I was looking for, labeled photo albums/memorabilia. I pulled out the albums, the yearbooks, and at the very bottom, my college honors hood. I had been comforted by the letter, but I also wanted it well out of my sight. I tucked it in one of the photo albums I'd taken with me when I left Bobbie's house, when photo albums were still physical, things you carted from place to place and added to as the years went by. When I tried to get everything back in the box, the unwieldy photo album slipped from my hands, landing on its spine and popped a few photographs from the cheap, plastic film, the glue beneath it long turned yellow and dry.

A photo of Mariah was face up on the ground. She wore a white nightgown and seemed to be peeking out from a blanket fort. Bobbie's house, I could tell, based on the high ceilings, the big window behind her curtainless, looking out into dark. I remembered the night because I'd brought my new camera to Bobbie's and wanted to practice my skills. I took photo after photo of Mariah, Bobbie, and Cassandra and found that only five pictures came out, none of Cassandra and only one of Bobbie. That night, I'd surprised Mariah as she was reading with a flashlight. The harsh light of it threw shadows on one side of Mariah's face, a sharp clarity on the other.

She'd been reading *The Once and Future King*, which she'd taken from Bobbie's bookshelf. She brought it home with her as well and read it often.

"Listen to this," Mariah had said just after I captured the photo. She'd barely seemed to register that I had taken her picture, which had irritated me: at the time, I was convinced that I had found my calling in photography and wanted everyone to know it, to acknowledge my talent. Mariah was too distracted, though, to notice.

"I love this," she said. "It's about Lancelot, who loves King Arthur as a friend and Guenever like a girlfriend. You know that cartoon *The Sword in the Stone*? The beginning is like that but the rest gets really weird. It's got a unicorn and these three brothers with a terrible mother who they love anyway. It's too much to explain, but let me read this part to you —

> He loved Arthur and he loved Guenever and he hated himself. The best knight of the world: everybody envied the self-esteem which must surely be his. But Lancelot never believed he was good or nice. Under the grotesque, magnificent shell with a face like Quasimodo's, there was shame and self-loathing which had been planted there when he was tiny, by something which it is now too late to trace. It is so fatally easy to make young children believe that they are horrible."

Something about the words hit me so hard that I couldn't speak. I almost felt angry at Mariah, but the feeling was so peculiar that I couldn't express it. I wasn't angry, I know now, but I felt exposed.

"That's kinda sad," I'd said, simply, wishing I had better words.

She nodded, watching me. I think she was waiting for me to say more. Waiting for me to tell her why it was sad, what it meant to me, what I understood. I didn't do any of that, though. I just walked away, leaving her in that place of expectation.

My mind has dramatized this event more than I should. I have highlighted my failure, but nothing that came after it. The truth is, after watching an episode of *The X-Files*, I wandered back into the bedroom and she read more to me. She read about Arthur, at the end of his life, wondering if he'd succeeded at all, realizing that he'd brought about his own ruin. Then, we'd stayed up talking until Bobbie came in and made us turn the lights off and go to bed.

In my mind, I'd highlighted it as a moment of failure. And maybe it was, but it was nestled among moments of connection. It would feel better to be able to point to a particular moment and say there, that's when it happened. That's when I first messed up, that's where she got a little crack of damage, and it made room for everything that came later.

This is revisionist history. I never was as powerful as I imagined and events moved around me, shaping themselves both in my presence and absence.

I took the photograph with me down to the living room, where I searched for a spot to put it. There, among a crowded table full of photographs, I placed it, resting gently against a photograph of me on the day I graduated from college. I wouldn't leave her here forever, out in the public eye for everyone to see, but right now I needed to see her as she had been, before the loneliness came over us both and sent us hurtling away from each other in opposite directions until we could no longer see each other, could no longer even speak each other's language.

Acknowledgments

Thank you to the entire Agape Editions/Haunted Doll House team, particularly Fox Henry Frazier for your editorial help and friendship.

Thank you to my early readers, including Chris Wells, K.D. Lovgren, Josh Hanson and Richard Thomas, who gave me invaluable feedback and advice to help me shape this book into something I'm proud of.

Thanks to The Writers' Colony at Dairy Hollow in Eureka Springs for providing space to complete the work, and to Zach Trent, for booking me weekend stays because I never remember to book them myself.

About the Author

Letitia Trent is the author of three novels, including *Summer Girls* and *Almost Dark*, and two full-length poetry collections. Her poetry and short stories have most recently appeared in *Biscuit Hill*, *Figure 1*, *Alice Says Go Fuck Yourself*, and *Smartish Pace*. Her short story "Wilderness" was nominated for a Shirley Jackson Award and later appeared in *Best Horror of the Year, Volume 8*. She lives in a haunted Ozark mountain town with her family and works in the mental health field. She can be reached via her substack, *Tell Me Something Good*, or Bluesky.

HAUNTED DOLL
HOUSE

Haunted Doll House is an imprint of Agape Editions. As our name suggests, we aren't afraid of the dark: we live there. We want your horror stories, your mystery novels, your dark sf/f, your genre-resistant writing about the ecstasies, traumas, & terrors that took you to the very edges of yourself.

AGAPE
EDITIONS

Agape Editions is a literary micropress created in southern California, now located in upstate New York. We publish visionary literature.

Our name comes from the ancient Greek ἀγάπη (agápē), describing the joyous love that exists universally without seeking or expecting anything in return. Agape can be described as the bond between humans & the Numinous, but we believe it exists everywhere — manifested through the kindness of strangers, felt alone under a sky filled with aurora, made real through a moment of ecstatic meditation or deep connection with another.

A moment of Agape is a moment in which you feel yourself fully — in the broader context of the universe at large.

Agape is about finding the strength & courage to remain open-hearted, in a world that doesn't always encourage or reward an open heart.

Our notions of the sacred & the Numinous span wide swaths of experience — private epiphanies; shared ecstasies; moments of intimacy; sublime revelation; cultural identity; spiritual traditions as conduit for survival. The psychic, the occult, the supernatural. The divinity of the natural world. Wild love. Fascinating scientific discovery. Mind-blowing technological advancement. Fernweh. The thrill of exploration. Sacred feminine rage.

We are profoundly uninterested in attempting to dictate the parameters of spiritual experience. We want to feel through you & your writing what's holy to you & why.

Imagine: awakening, breathless, in the thick of night. You've been dreaming of William Blake's Tyger-burning-bright & all its terrifying beauty. & now, from somewhere in the surrounding darkness, you can hear its quiet breathing.

Welcome to Agape Editions.